SHERLOCK HOLMES:

The Pearl of Death
And Other Early Stories

GC Rosenquist

Paperback ISBN 9781780927367
ePub ISBN 978-1-78092-737-4
PDF ISBN 978-1-78092-738-1

Published in the UK by MX Publishing
335 Princess Park Manor, Royal Drive,
London, N11 3GX
www.mxpublishing.co.uk

Cover design by www.staunch.com

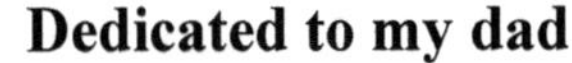

Dedicated to my dad

CONTENTS:

THE PEARL OF DEATH

Holmes and I were first made aware of the theft of the Pearl of Death by means of the front page of the Friday morning *London Gazette*.

The sole property of the Philippine government, it had secretly come in to the Shadwell docks on a steamer named the *Valiant* for the purpose of display in the National Gallery. The Pearl of Death was a giant natural pearl, the largest ever discovered, coming to some fifteen pounds in weight and over nine inches in diameter. It was found in the throat of a giant oyster that resided in the waters around the Philippine island of Palawan. The diver that first set eyes on the pearl drowned when the cockles of the mighty mollusk closed in on his hand as he reached for it and, the Gazette explained, every owner of the pearl since had died under mysterious circumstance, perhaps by means of an inexplicable curse. Hence the name, Pearl of Death.

"Bah!" I exclaimed from my chair across from Holmes, in our comfortable parlour on 221b Baker Street. "If this pearl is such a horrible thing, why should it come to England?"

"It's a rarity, Watson," Holmes answered, his eyes never leaving the lines of text on the paper. Blue tufts of scented smoke came up from the button of a pipe that hung from his thin mouth. "It's unique. People have never seen a pearl the size of a man's head before. And the hint of a silly curse makes it all the more tantalizing."

"So you make nothing of the curse then?"

"Of course not, Watson. And neither should you. Belief in a curse is the sign of a low thinking, superstitious man. We are not in the dark ages any more, my friend."

I nodded in agreement. "So what could a bloody thing like that be worth?"

Holmes read on for a moment, then answered: "It says here it has been appraised at three and a half million pounds."

"Good god, Holmes!" I thundered, nearly swallowing my morning cheroot.

Holmes glanced up at me and grinned. "Quite, my dear Watson. I expect we'll be getting the call from Scotland Yard any moment now."

As if his words were an actor's prompt in a play, our landlady Mrs. Hudson, opened the door and informed us that Detective Inspector Lestrade from Scotland Yard has arrived and was asking for an audience.

***

It was a surprisingly easy task to track down the Pearl of Death once Holmes put his exceptionally swift deductive talents to the test. The difficulty came in actually securing it.

The first thing Holmes and I did was to take a cab for the Shadwell district in the East End, where the docks were, to talk to the captain of the *Valiant*. It appeared that the Pearl of Death was too large to fit in the ship's safe so the Captain ordered that it be placed in a non-descript leather shoulder bag and stored down in the storage compartment with the other items of trade. It was his opinion that the more it resembled everything else down there, the less chance it would be recognized and pinched. He had been proven incorrect in his assertion and now he stood before us, hunched over and perspiring as if a ton of great worry had been lowered upon his shoulders. He was surely to be relieved of duty, and possibly thrown in prison, should the pearl never be recovered.

Holmes asked for and received the crew manifest whereas he promptly noticed that only one crew member hadn't signed out for forty-eight hour liberty, Joseph Wayne Thornwald.

"That's our man!" Holmes said confidently.

"But are you sure, Mr Holmes?" the Captain asked.

"Criminals often display tunnel vision while committing their crimes, they forget to perform even the most rudimentary tasks that would forever cover their tracks. That's what happened here. The absence of his signature on the liberty manifest is as good as a confession."

"If you are correct," the Captain began. "Take great care when approaching him, for he is a man of monstrous height, temper and strength. He's been our best coal stoker for ten years."

"There is the motive for the crime, Captain," Holmes said. "Ten years is a long time to shovel coal into the hellish boiler furnaces of a trade steamer. Thornwald saw the pearl as a chance to make a single monetary windfall that would set him up for life, free him from his daily purgatory. And considering the fact that the storage compartments are one level above the boiler rooms, Thornwald had ample knowledge and opportunity to pinch the pearl. Rest easy, Captain, we'll get the pearl back and you'll be spared imprisonment."

Once outside we took a cab back to the financial district of Central London, to the establishments of five possible black market buyers Holmes was familiar with, only one of which acknowledged he'd met the aforementioned Joseph Thornwald. The buyer, recognizing the pearl, realizing it had been stolen and knowing its true value, had turned Thornwald down cold. No one, it seemed, was willing to pony up the three and a half million pounds for the chance to die mysteriously by curse or risk being imprisoned. Thornwald was never going to be able to sell the pearl while in England so it became even more urgent for us to find him before he booked passage out of the country on a different East End steamer.

Holmes, more resolute than ever, put the dependable children of his *Baker Street Irregulars* on the case. A shilling to the one who discovered Thornwald's location. So, all over the squalid rookeries and pubs of the East End an army of street urchins flitted about, asking questions, peeking into the windows of locals, frequenting pubs, while Holmes and I took up headquarters in the St Paul Church on Fox Lane. And it worked. In an hour, as Holmes and I were finishing a smoke, young Peter Lawson rushed into the church vestibule and told us that there was a freakishly big man wearing a leather bag around his shoulder, having a pint in *The Red Rabbit*, a pub on Little Spring Street not a stone's throw from the church.

"The man is having a pint in a pub while holding a stolen object worth three and a half million pounds?" I asked incredulously. "The arrogance!"

"Not arrogance, my friend," Holmes corrected. "Pure, unadulterated ignorance. I expected this. Must I remind you that Thornwald's only skill and education has been in shoveling coal?"

Of course, Holmes was right. He had a way of putting things clear in my mind that should have been obvious to me from the start.

"Peter," Holmes called. The boy rushed up to him and Holmes put a hand on his small shoulder. "Go and fetch the constables that patrol this district. Tell them what you know."

The small, dirty-faced boy held out an open hand and Holmes dropped two shillings into it, instead of one. The boy smiled in surprise, made a fist, turned and ran away on a pair of filthy bare feet.

"Hurry, Watson!" Holmes shouted as he checked the loaded chambers of his pistol. Then he rushed outside. "Our luck is hot, we must strike fast!"

***

"Give it up, Thornwald!" Holmes ordered, the barrel of his pistol was pointed at the unbelievably large man. "I don't wish to shoot you, but I will if you force me to."

We had chased Thornwald out of the pub, through the shabbiest alleys and dens of Shadwell and now had him cornered on the weathered roof of a brick tenement on New Street. I could see all of Shadwell from there, its landscape was black and jagged, like an old man's teeth, under the darkening cherry red sky. Behind us, cutting through the black, jagged landscape like a glowing red ribbon of blood was the Thames. Sailing cutters with their sails down and steamers with their bellies empty of fire sat moored and quiet on both shores. Night was coming fast.

The roof was large and pitched slightly to the east, in some places it moved when stepped upon. I had distinct visions of falling through, killing myself five stories below. The roofs of the neighbouring tenements were shingle-covered A-frame structures and appeared just as dangerous.

There were communal chimneys made of aged red brick standing in each corner of our roof, the mortar between the bricks of each had dried out and cracked away in some places, giving the chimneys the warped look of a patient's spine with scoliosis. Strung between the two chimneys on the east side was a thick clothesline where various bits of hosiery and undergarments hung, wafting lightly in the breeze. Pitting the roof every few feet, and probably further weakening it, sprouted the cylindrical metal tips of plumber's vents. Above and behind us stood a massive water tower perched upon four wooden legs, each of which held the obvious signs of termite decay, it seemed to me the water tower could come down at any moment.

I tell you truthfully, I was more frightful of the roof than I was of the lumbering giant before us.

Thornwald stood there like a stone monolith, every bit of seven feet tall. His shoulders were massive, nearly as wide as he was tall, his thick, stump-like legs were spread apart, ready to spring. He wore a clean blue blouse, black opened vest and black breeches that fell effortlessly into a pair of shiny black leather boots. His hands hung suspended to his sides, fingers splayed open, capable of engulfing my whole head. His fingernails were ringed black with coke at the cuticles, the only clue that betrayed what his true vocation was. His muscular head was covered with short, sweaty, curled black hair and sat directly on his shoulders, dismissing the need for anything that resembled a neck. His eyes were dark and deep set, framed by a pair of thick, bushy eyebrows. His nose was long and proportional, his mouth thin but wide. Around steel cut jowls clung the brown leather straps belonging to the leather bag that carried the Pearl of Death.

Holmes, against my bitter prodding, took a step forward, his pistol still trained on Thornwald. "Look around you. There's no escape," he said. "Give me the pearl, Thornwald. I promise you a fair trial. You'll be released and rehabilitated in five years."

Thornwald's eyes went from me, then to Holmes, then repeated the process. I could see the machinery clicking behind his eyes as he weighed every option of escape. A few minutes before, as we rushed up the stairs leading to the roof, Holmes suggested a bold plan of attack should Thornwald decide to fight us before the police arrived. He said that big men tire easy, they have no persistence in their general make-up, so we should cling to him like hungry children cling to their mother, add more weight to his already stressed frame. Then, when the time arrives, one of us should distract him while the other pinches the pearl. The plan seemed sound and in the absence of anything else, I went for it.

Well, Thornwald decided to fight us. In one stunningly quick and graceful movement, he brought his right hand about, grabbed up the leather bag and swung it forward, knocking the pistol from Holmes' hand. The pistol spun through the air and disappeared down over the roof edge. We were so far up I couldn't hear it hit the ground. It was then that I cursed at myself for forgetting to bring my service revolver.

I shot a quick glance at Holmes. His eyes were narrowed, his brows were together, a sly grin creased his thin face. He seemed to me the perfect picture of an eagle on the hunt. “Marvelous!” he exclaimed through a half-laugh, then he jumped up on to the giant, his arms locked securely around Thornwald’s protruding jowls.

In surprise, Thornwald stepped back, brought his hands up, grabbed Holmes by the waist and began pushing him away. But Holmes wouldn’t budge, his grip remained solid. They struggled for some seconds before I realized that Holmes was urging me on to do as he had done. I ran around and jumped on to Thornwald’s back, but the only thing my delicate doctor’s hands could gain purchase of was Holmes’ elbows. Thornwald released a series of strained grunts, his boots stomping heavily upon the uncertain surface of the roof as the three of us spun in wild circles. Then, one of those plumber’s vents got in Thornwald’s way and he tripped, sending us rolling upon the roof like spilled marbles.

When the three of us gained footing again, we found our positions had reversed. Thornwald was now standing in front of the deteriorated wooden legs of the water tower.

“Let’s ram him,” Holmes murmured into my ear.

"Ram him?" I repeated stupidly. "Are you mad, Holmes? Those wooden legs will snap like match sticks under Thornwald's weight."

Again, Holmes flashed that sly grin. "I'm counting on it, dear Watson. It will make for the perfect distraction," he said then counted to three. We sprinted across the roof as fast as our young legs allowed, skillfully avoiding the trip traps of the plumber's vents while doing so and when we hit Thornwald's chest, our momentum was enough only to move him back one step. But that was enough. Thornwald backed into the northwestern leg of the water tower. It gave out an ear-splitting crack as it broke apart, then the lower portion of it spun and bounced upon the roof's tarred surface. But, to my disbelief, the tower remained standing on its three remaining legs.

As Holmes and I got to our feet again, Thornwald looked up at the tower, let out a single victorious guffaw, then faced us, a dark leer tattooed on his face.

"What do we do now, Holmes?" I asked.

"Run at the tower, Watson," Holmes replied. "Out of the way of the tsunami."

I glanced at the tower, it didn't seem to be going anywhere and I surely didn't want to be in near proximity of that angry giant. Had Holmes committed a rare error? Noticing my reticence, Holmes grabbed my arm and pulled me forward. "Come on, man!" he shouted and I blindly ran after him.

Thornwald saw us coming and leaned forward, bracing for another attack, but Holmes took a wide path around him and laid his right shoulder into the northeast tower leg as he ran by. It came apart in a flash of splinters and wood dust, the bottom half of the leg joined the other severed remnant on the roof. Holmes and I ducked and rolled, smashing into the wall of the south side of the roof, almost directly under the water tower. Above us, the two remaining rear legs, unable to support the great weight of the water tower, snapped off in the middle, sounding like a pair of bullet blasts as the tower, holding thousands of gallons of collected rainwater, fell forward.

The normal tick of time appeared to slow as it came down. The rusty conical reservoir cap opened like a great yawning mouth, vomiting long, wide, heavy streams of fresh rainwater. Thornwald turned around and stared up at the oncoming doom, his face screwed into a mask of sheer horror, then some low part of the tower itself hit him in the head, he went down faster than the tower. When the tower hit the roof, it was like the detonation of a thousand pound explosion, the entire structure of the building shuddered under the impact. For a brief instant Holmes and I were thrown up into the air, nearly flying off the roof as we came down. On my hands and knees, I watched as the contents of the great water tower spilled out across the roof, the sound of rolling thunder filled my ears with such force I had to cover them with my hands. A great dark wave of immense proportions rolled forth, striking the brick wall of the north end of the roof, sweeping it away as if the bricks had been made of paper. The path of the rushing water continued forward, splashing on to the facing, shingled field of the A-frame roof of the neighboring tenement, where it exploded in a spray of white froth, spinning the weathered arms of a nearby weathervane, then fell some five stories to the ground. Hopefully, no one had been standing down there when it all came down.

Amazingly, those sick, twisted chimneys in the corner of the roof remained unharmed, catching some of the water runoff and sending it back our way where it swept across Thornwald's limp body. The cool water must have had a reinvigorating effect on our quarry, because he started to moan and move his legs.

Holmes leapt to his feet, rushed over to the groggy giant and stripped him of the bag, then he put the straps around his neck and shoulder. Somewhere below, I heard panicked voices and police whistles echoing. Holmes, also alerted, went over to the side of the roof and waved at them. "Hurry up, Detective Inspector! Before this monster fully awakes!" he shouted.

But it was too late. As Holmes was shouting at Detective Inspector Lestrade, Thornwald had risen to his hands and knees, shook heavy beads of cool water from his curled locks and felt around for his precious bag. Realizing it was gone, he stood up, looked at me, noticed I didn't have the bag, then turned back towards Holmes.

"No!" the beast cried. "It's mine!" He took one step towards Holmes and without thinking of the ramifications of my actions, I was quickly upon his back again, trying to give Holmes time for an escape. While Thornwald struggled with me I watched as Holmes started for the door to the roof's access shaft, but Thornwald and I were blocking it. So, Holmes turned and in three strides, he leapt for the roof of the neighboring tenement. He hit the facing roof field and because it was still wet with fresh water, he slipped, nearly sliding off the edge. Luckily, that weathervane was within his reach and he grabbed it, pulling himself up to the crest of the roof and to safety.

Thornwald had also seen this and, furious, he grabbed my wrist, throwing me off his back. The only thing that saved me from a long fall was that clothesline. It stretched under my weight but held, snapping me back on to the roof.

Thornwald moved with surprising swiftness, trying to repeat what Holmes had done. His huge, heavy legs successfully propelled him across the short distance to the other roof, but the combination of his weight and the subtle damage the wave of onrushing water had caused upon the roof a minute before was too much for the underlying structure. Thornwald went through the shingles like a falling meteor, disappearing almost as soon his boots made contact. His frantic wail faded as he crashed through floor after floor. In a breath, all that remained of Thornwald's presence was smoke and dust streaming up through the hole he'd made.

Tired, sore and drenched, I hobbled over to the edge of the roof, glanced over at the hole then up at Holmes, who stood there perfectly at ease, his hand grasping the weathervane. "Good show, Watson," he said. "Thank you for your assistance. You saved the case."

"Clever of you…to use the weakened roof…against him," I said, almost breathlessly. "I never…would have thought of that."

"Thankfully, neither did he," Holmes said. "Now stand aside, my friend, I'm coming back over."

***

"I-I say, Holmes," I stammered, staring at the abomination sitting inside the leather bag. The Pearl of Death resembled more a white, fossilized coprolite rather than a giant, shining, lustrous pearl. "It looks nothing like any pearl I've ever seen."

"That's why its value is so great, Watson," Holmes stated as he closed the bag and handed it over to Detective Inspector Lestrade. "It took that deadly mollusk over a hundred years of constant irritation at the bottom of the sea to create something so large. The chances of finding another one like it are almost nil. It's priceless really."

The grunts of a dozen men brought our attention to the open door of a nearby tenement. Thornwald's massive broken body was being carried out by six constables on each side, to an oversized flat cart sitting nearby. Groups of locals, adults and children and dogs, were standing around watching the spectacle.

"It appears the curse of the Pearl of Death certainly worked against Thornwald, wouldn't you say, Holmes?" I prodded jokingly.

“Hmmm. Perhaps, Watson,” Holmes agreed, surprising me to the marrow. “Maybe if he threw some salt over his shoulder or kissed a horseshoe I never would have spotted the absence of his name on the liberty manifest. And maybe I wouldn’t have been able to trace him from London’s financial district to the Red Rabbit Pub, or-“

“Point taken, Holmes,” I said, utterly defeated by my try at dry humor.

“Then let’s get some dinner, dear Watson. I’m completely famished.”

MRS WATSON'S GOLD LOCKET

"I was robbed, Holmes!" I ejaculated suddenly. "I was robbed, I tell you!"

It was a cool, overcast evening. Holmes and I were strolling north along Baker Street, completing our after supper walk. I was enjoying a fresh cheroot and he dangled a well-used pipe from his mouth as if it were a worm on a fish hook. He refrained from looking at me but my sudden outburst had clearly troubled him.

"Have you informed Scotland Yard, Watson?" Holmes asked with much concern in his voice. He stared at the ground as we walked, the often familiar form he took while silently performing mental exercises.

"No, no, Holmes," I answered, removing the cheroot from between my teeth. "I thought this a case best suited to your talents."

He nodded, swung his walking stick up so that it held securely in his armpit, then, his full attention focused on my predicament, he glanced at me finally. "Do tell me the story, if you will, Watson," he said, rising up to the challenge. "And be sure to relay every detail."

"Quite, quite," I said. "It happened back in '80, while I was serving her Majesty's forces during the Second Anglo-Afghan war."

"Yes," Holmes recalled. "In Maiwand. You were wounded, took a Jezail bullet in the shoulder."

"Right," I said, then continued my story. "As I convalesced day after day on the dreary cot of a hospital ward in Peshawur, I was under the care of a young, skilled nurse by the name of Julia. Her hair was long and curled, the color of rose petals in full bloom, matching her lips. Her face was white and as unblemished as a China doll. Her bedside manner was delightful and it seemed she lavished upon me more attention than she did the other poor lads barracked with me."

"Oh, come now, Watson," Holmes interrupted skeptically. "She was a nurse, it's their job to make you feel that way. The better and quicker to get you up and on your feet."

"I understand that, Holmes," I retorted. "But I was a rather dashing and fit figure before the Afghan conflict, strong and virile of youth. I had very little trouble meeting women. I know it may seem ridiculous as you look at me now but, she really did offer more of her time to me than with the others. For example, she read excerpts from the good book to me every night before the candles were blown out. I never once saw her reading to the other lads while I was there. And she always let me have a small nip of brandy after lunch-"

"She never let the others have a taste?" Holmes asked.

"Why, yes, of course she did, Holmes," I replied. "But she never stayed and shared a glass with them as she did with me. She would slide my feet over, sit down on the cot and talk with me. It was during this time we would reveal details about our lives back home in England. She was welsh but had obvious Irish ancestry. Her father and mother owned a sheep farm near the coast. She had a younger brother, still in school at the time."

"Did she have a beau?"

"She never mentioned one but it always occurred to me that a girl with her unmistakable beauty would be like a light to moths, attracting every man within seeing distance. In fact, some of the other lads would say the most derogatory things about her after she finished her rounds and left the ward, but I never joined in with them, even when they prodded me like a gang of school children. All of this behaviour was undoubtedly brought on by jealousy so I ignored them."

"Good for you, Watson."

“Thank you, Holmes. But what really made me think Julia had true feelings for me was this…each of us had a small lock box placed under the cot to house items of a personal nature. Most of the others only kept letters from home inside the box, or cigarettes. I, however, kept a small pocket Bible and something else very close to my heart…a gold locket with a painted picture of my late mother inside it. She passed away when I was very young so I had very few memories of her. When I joined her Majesty’s forces, my father gave me the locket as a gesture of good luck. It was all I had left of her. To keep the dogs of depression away while I recuperated, I always held the locket in my hand, that way I could open it up whenever I wanted and my mother’s beauty would always cheer me up.”

“Hmmm,” Holmes ruminated. “And how does this locket relate to Julia?”

“Well, she noticed the intense pain and discomfort I had to fight through in my shoulder as I reached down, opened the lock box and pulled the locket out in the morning, and she noticed it was the same in the evening when I put it back into the lock box. So she took it upon herself to perform that chore for me…every morning it was the first thing she did and every evening it was the last thing she did. Very touching, really, Holmes."

"I'm sure."

"Then I contracted enteric fever and she doubled her efforts over my comfort. As I lay there sweltering, dying, she put the locket into my hand…every morning. And took it away every night. She read to me, kept my brow covered with a cold wet towel to bring my fever down, fed me broth to keep my strength up. She never left my side, ignoring the other responsibilities she had towards the other lads. I didn't feel I deserved the sort of attention she was giving me but I loved it just the same."

"You are only human, Watson."

"Quite right, Holmes. Thank you for noticing."

"Judging by the fact that you're here walking and talking with me now, you recovered fully." This was his attempt at speeding the story up.

"Quite right again, Holmes," I said. "Thanks to Julia's obsessive care and my will to live for her. But my injury, combined with the recent illness I'd just recovered from left me weak and emaciated, knocking me out of her Majesty's forces. I had orders to return to England on the *HMS Orontes* in a week. This caused me a mountain of anxiety as I was completely, utterly under Julia's spell and didn't want to leave her. I had fantasies of the both of us returning home, getting married, buying a home, raising children, all the rest. This whole wonderful future was before me. So when I told her I'd received my orders and was going home, I asked her to marry me. She stood there like a piece of marble, staring at me as if my hair had suddenly caught fire. 'Oh, dear,' she said. 'I-I can't marry you, John. I'm already married. His name is Rickenbocker. He's leading her Majesty's forces up in Maiwand. I'm so sorry if I led you to believe-' I couldn't hear the rest of what she'd said because I knew this Rickenbocker, he was the man who led the charge in which I'd gotten wounded. The pointed arrowhead of irony hit me square in the gut, Holmes, and I felt immediately sick again. Sick and humiliated. I couldn't wait seven days, I made passage for the *HMS Orontes* immediately, without my dignity and my heart. It was just as you'd said…she was a nurse doing her job. I was too young and inexperienced to realize it."

Holmes stopped walking, stared down at the sidewalk again in concentrated silence, thinking the whole story through. Then he looked up at me, his face a puzzle of confusion. "So, it wasn't until you were well on your way home to England that you'd discovered Julia had robbed you of your mother's gold locket?"

I hesitated a moment, then nodded. I remembered I'd begun the story by claiming I'd been robbed, forcing his brilliant mind to focus in on my mother's locket as if a possible crime had been committed against it. So, expecting to solve a crime, he'd completely misunderstood the story I was telling him.

I didn't have the desire to tell my good friend, Sherlock Holmes, that what Julia had truly stolen from me was my innocence.

MYSTERY OF THE NAMELESS MAN

"You must help me, Mr Holmes!" the man sitting in the chair pleaded in a distinctly Scottish accent. "It's been three days and I still don't know who I am!"

He was an older, stoutly built man with a pair of large bulbous eyes protruding from under a brow completely naked of eyebrows. There was a purple, slightly swollen, oval-shaped bruise on his right temple. An uneven, patchy, thinly veiled mustache was trimmed tightly above his upper lip. His brown hair was thin and frizzy in front but thick and wavy in back. His face was round and wide and carried the unmistakable pink shadows of rosacea on his cheeks, chin and forehead. His nose, also stained pink, was flattish, with thin nostrils. His hands were large and heavy with thick fingers that seemed unnaturally tanned on the knuckles, except on his ring finger where a white halo was plainly evident where a wedding band used to be. His big hands moved around in quick, frantic movements as he talked. He wore a brown dress suit that looked as if he'd slept in it, wrinkled at the elbows and knees, stained and unkempt in other areas. In his breast pocket was a brightly colored plaid handkerchief of black, red and yellow.

His black leather shoes had thick soles on them and would have presented nicely after a much needed shine.

Detective Inspector Lestrade stood behind the man, listening as he warmed his hands free of the late January chill in the newly stoked fire of our Baker Street hearth. He'd brought the man to us only a few moments before, just after our evening meal, obviously frustrated that he couldn't help the man even with all the resources of Scotland Yard behind him. Coming to see Holmes was, as always, a last resort.

Holmes sat in his armchair, long legs crossed, fingertips pressed together at his chin. His dark, penetrating eyes narrowed intensely and his mouth became a granite-like slit as he listened to the nameless man tell his tale.

"Three days!" the man repeated, his voice was on the verge of breaking.

"And what happened to you three days ago, sir?" Holmes asked.

"Th-that's just it, Mr Holmes…I don't know. All I know is that I woke up in a forest with the morning light blinding my eyes and my head throbbing. My surroundings were perfectly alien to me, I might have been standing on the moon for all I knew. Even more horrible was that I couldn't remember who I was. A quick check for a billfold upon my person revealed nothing."

"You'd been attacked and robbed," Holmes stated confidently. "Resulting in acute amnesia."

"It-it would appear so, Mr Holmes," the man said, then continued. "By a band of thieves desperate for treasure. So, frightened, battered and lost, I panicked and ran, luckily coming to a road a few minutes later that cut north and south through the forest. It looked a well-traveled avenue so I followed it south, hoping I would come across someone who could tell me where I was. But my bad luck continued, because for half a day I walked, thirsty and hungry, meeting no one until I reached the outskirts of what I later learned to be London. A rider on a horse heading north met me and saw my poor condition. He was good enough to take me to Scotland Yard where, for three days, none of the inspectors have been able puzzle out my situation. I've been staying in a hospital with only the clothes I'm wearing to suffice. Do you know how unsettling it is, Mr Holmes, not to know who or where you are or why you're even here?"

Holmes nodded. "It must be very disorientating for you," he said.

“To say the least!” the man exploded, then apologized for his outburst.

“Think nothing of it, my good man,” Holmes said calmly. “I understand your emotional state of mind completely. You are not to be held accountable.”

“Th-thank you, sir.”

Lestrade removed himself from in front of the hearth and pulled up a chair from our dining room table. He sat down with a sigh and looked at Holmes. “Well, what do you think, Mr Holmes? Can you help him?” he asked. From Lestrade’s haughty tone, I got the impression that this was a challenge to Holmes’ method of investigation, as if he’d finally brought the famous consulting detective a mystery he couldn’t solve.

Holmes reached over, grabbed his pipe from the side table, lit it then took a couple thoughtful puffs. From all this hesitation, I’d nearly concluded that Lestrade’s assumption may have been correct. Then, after re-lighting the bowl of his pipe, Holmes finally replied. “Of course I can help him, Detective Inspector. Everything you need to know to solve this gentleman’s case is sitting right there before you.” Holmes, using his pipe, pointed at the poor nameless man. “Not only can I tell you his name, I can tell you exactly where he’s from, what line of work he’s in, that he’s married, which forest he was left for dead in three days ago, and that he knew his attacker."

"I did?" the nameless man asked incredulously.

"Yes," Holmes answered. "In fact, my friend, you were never supposed to leave that forest alive."

Lestrade crossed his arms defiantly. "Unbelievable, even for you, Holmes!" he exclaimed.

"Skeptical? Shall I walk you through it then, Mr Lestrade?" Holmes asked rhetorically and began a most remarkable narrative. "We'll begin with the mysterious forest our client here woke up in the morning after his attack. There are five major forests north of London but which one was it? Sir, you said that you'd walked half a day until you reached London, the only forest north of London that's half a day's travel on foot is Waltham Forest. This is important to know because, due to the heavy Scottish accent you carry, it's clear you were traveling south from somewhere in Scotland and every traveler coming from there usually goes through Waltham Forest. But where in Scotland are you from? I'd say a positive guess is the Nairn region, directly northeast of Loch Ness."

"B-but how could you know that?" the nameless man asked.

"Your handkerchief, sir," Holmes answered. He reached over, pinched it from the man's coat pocket and held it up for us to see. It was a plaid patterned wool cloth; thick black bands over a red field with a thin yellow line running through the bands. "The tartan of the Brodie Clan," Holmes explained as he got up from his chair, went over to the bookshelf, pulled a rather heavy volume from the shelf and paged through it until he came across the page he wanted. Then he handed both the tartan and the volume over to the nameless man. The golden embossed title on the spine read *"Historical Tartans of Ancient Scottish Clans."* Holmes continued: "Brodie…one of Scotland's most ancient clans, located in the Nairn region. Most Scottish travelers wear some form of their clan's identification when they leave their native lands. You probably wore a hat with a band of the same design but your attacker stole it."

The man brought his hands up to his head. "I wore a hat?" he asked.

"Yes, but he forgot to take the handkerchief, which tells me that your attacker wasn't a professional."

"It wasn't a band of thieves then, Mr Holmes?" the man asked.

"I'm afraid not, sir. The whole crime was made to look as if they had perpetrated it, though. You must remember, it's late January, much too cold a time for thieves to be prowling the forests of England. Secondly, you have only one bruise on your right temple, a band of attackers would have left you unrecognizable with bruises, then finished you off with a blade to the jugular or straight through the heart. No, you were accosted by one person, someone you knew."

"How can you know this, Holmes?" Lestrade asked.

"Two clues, Detective Inspector," Holmes replied. "The fact that the attacker stole this man's hat, is one. He knew that the tartan band on the hat could be traced back to Nairn and the last thing the attacker wanted was inspectors from Scotland Yard snooping around there. Next, the oval-shaped bruise on this man's temple clearly indicates the tool of attack was the butt of a hunting rifle, which means that the attacker had to get close enough to this man in order to do the deed." Holmes' glance focused on the nameless man. "I would surmise, sir, that you had a male riding companion traveling to London with you."

"Why didn't the attacker shoot him?" Lestrade asked.

"Thieves in Waltham forest don't murder people with hunting rifles, Detective Inspector. The attacker, covering his identity, knew this and proceeded accordingly."

"But I don't remember any of this!" the man cried.

"Not to worry. If your amnesia turns out to be temporary, you'll remember all of it in good time, sir."

"But why was he and this companion traveling to London in the first place, Holmes?" Lestrade asked.

"Could be any number of reasons, Lestrade. Perhaps it was a planned holiday, or maybe a visit to a dying relative. My suspicion is that it has something to do with this man's profession."

"Which is?"

"He's a lighthouse keeper, has been for a very long time."

"Explain yourself, Holmes," Lestrade urged. His voice was tinged with frustration as he saw his victory over Holmes being dashed away ever so cleverly with every succeeding deduction.

"Look at the man's face, Lestrade, it's plainly obvious," Holmes said. "See the rosacea on his nose and cheeks, that's actually windburn from facing the stiff winter winds coming in off the North Sea. Notice how his eyebrows are missing, the hair on his forehead is singed, his mustache is patchy from heat? Notice his fingers and how unnaturally tanned they are? You can clearly see the white area around his ring finger where a wedding band, now stolen, used to be. Some of the nightly tasks a lighthouse keeper is charged with is seeing that the oil in the lamp is full and then there's the hazardous lighting of the wick…the rush of heat the keeper is exposed to night after night is equivalent to the heat coming from a blast furnace, resulting in the aforementioned symptoms I've just exposed for you. Then there are his shoes, the kind only a lighthouse keeper wears, thickly soled for scaling a long spiral staircase consisting of hundreds of steps. One final clue confirmed it for me, though…the fact that he said he was blinded by the morning light in the forest, hinting at a common malady most lighthouse keepers share after many years on the job; a sensitivity to light, even from the dim morning light in a forest. I'd say this man keeps the lighthouse at Lossiemouth, in the Moray Firth, very near Nairn, and has been doing so for two decades or more."

"Incredible! But my name, Mr Holmes!" the man interrupted impatiently. "You said you knew my name!"

"Yes, of course, sir," Holmes said. "Fortunately for us, the clan Brodie is associated with only two names; *Brodie* and

Bryde. It states as much in that book you're holding. I assume you are the latter as no one would dare kill off a person with the chief namesake of the clan. So, let's review the facts of your case: Your name is Bryde and you're married. You are a member of the ancient Scottish Brodie Clan and you come from the Nairn area of Scotland, where you have been a lighthouse keeper at Lossiemouth for two decades or more. You were traveling to London with a familiar acquaintance who, for nefarious but unknown reasons, attempted to murder you in cold blood, but instead, left you accidentally alive and burdened with a serious case of amnesia. Did I pass the exam, Mr Lestrade?"

The Detective Inspector flashed an angry, defeated look at Holmes. "Yes, Mr Holmes. Top of the class, as usual."

"You know all of this, Mr Holmes, yet you don't know the motive for my attempted murder?" Bryde asked. He seemed less emotional now that he had some solid answers to his predicament.

Holmes slipped his pipe into his mouth, sat down in the armchair again and spoke through his teeth. "I have my suspicions, of course, Mr Bryde, but I never guess when it comes to a motive. I'll need more facts first. Detective Inspector Lestrade must take you back up to Scotland, with a pair of constables in support, in order to find that out. Perhaps, during his investigation, you'll recover your memory completely and know the truth for yourself."

"Can you reveal to me your suspicions, at least?"

After a moment of deep contemplation, Holmes took the pipe out of his mouth. "I fear, Mr Bryde, that your wife can successfully close this case."

***

A week later, Lestrade visited us again at 221b Baker Street, freshly returned from his adventure in Scotland concerning the formerly nameless man, Mr Bryde.

"I must confess, Holmes," Detective Inspector Lestrade began, nursing a half empty glass of brandy while sitting in Holmes' armchair. "Your brain works like no other brain I know."

Holmes, lighting his pipe while standing near the flaming hearth, smiled. "I'll take that as a compliment, Mr Lestrade."

"Everything you said turned out to be true," Lestrade continued. "Bryde's name, member of the Brodie Clan, his occupation…twenty-six years as a lighthouse keeper at Lossiemouth, attacked in Waltham Forest, just as you'd said-"

"By his wife's lover?" Holmes interrupted.

Lestrade nodded. "Just as you'd figured. The man's name was McCurdle, one of Bryde's lighthouse assistants. Young, strong and virile sort. When Bryde, the two constables I'd brought along with me, and I went into the lighthouse, we caught Bryde's wife in bed with McCurdle. The look of surprise on their faces was one for the books!" Lestrade let out a quick laugh at the reminiscence. "Bryde's hat, billfold and wedding band were on the dresser, they'd had no idea they'd ever been suspected. It was then that Mr Bryde recovered full access to his memory."

"Shock will sometimes do that. And what was his trip to London about?"

"It was phony as an iron shilling, Holmes," Lestrade replied. "Bryde's wife had been putting it into his mind for a while that she was sick of living out there in that lighthouse, bored, isolated from everyone. She told him she wanted the bustle and excitement of city life so she urged him to find work in London so that they could move there. McCurdle, being a *true* friend, offered to go with him, keep him company, but the reality was that he wanted to shack up with Mrs Bryde and killing Mr Bryde in Waltham Forest, blaming thieves, was the best plan he could think up. It would have worked if not for you."

"I appreciate the sentiment, Mr Lestrade," Holmes said. "But if McCurdle had succeeded in murdering Bryde out there in that forest, no one would ever have found his body and-"

"Oh, for God's sake, Holmes!" I exclaimed. "Just accept the man's compliment. You never know when you'll get another one out of him!"

"Quite right, Watson," Holmes said. "Quite right."

LURE OF THE RHINOCEROS HEAD

It was on a dreary, rainy Monday morning, a morning riddled with the trembling's of thunder far off in the distance, Sherlock Holmes and I were called upon by Scotland Yard to help investigate, in Commissioner Carruther's own words, a *truly dastardly case of the murderous type.*

When we arrived at the gates of Gray's Inn Gardens, a small tree-filled park that had long winding brick walks cut through it, located a block north of the Royal Courts of Justice, there were two constables standing guard, forbidding public entrance into the park. But upon recognizing my esteemed friend, the constables snapped to attention and saluted, allowing us free egress through the gates, into the park.

A few strides inside the gates Holmes and I saw a constable standing guard over a rumpled black tarp covering the body of the poor victim lying on the walk. A pair of black stockinged feet stuck out of the tarp at one end, but the shiny black shoes the feet belonged to were sitting a few feet away, arranged as if the victim were still standing in them. The closer we approached the tarp, the heavier the odor of burnt flesh fell over my nostrils. Quite disagreeable. A handful of constables were scouring the immediate area for clues.

"Holmes!" came a rumbling voice and out from the shadows of a tree appeared Commissioner of Scotland Yard, Yancy Carruthers. His face was stern yet colorless in the stale, overcast light of the morning.

"Good to see you again, Commissioner," Holmes said as he shook the Commissioner's hand. "How can I help you this morning?"

Commissioner Carruthers cleared his throat, adjusted his coat and answered. "I have a bodge of a case here, Holmes," he began. "Come have a look."

The Commissioner led us to the rumpled black tarp, leaned over and pulled the tarp back, revealing the ghastly remains of what appeared to be a tall gentleman. The burnt odor was so strong I had to pull a handkerchief from my breast pocket and cover my nose with it.

"Steady, Watson," Holmes said then slowly fell to one knee to investigate the victim.

Everything above the man's knees was a black, charred, nearly unrecognizable mass. All that remained of his attire were two tattered and singed cylinders of gray wool slacks covering his shins, and of course, the black stockings on his feet. In the victim's right hand was a walking stick but it appeared to me that the flesh of the charred, black hand had been melted to the silver plated crown of the walking stick, which was designed in the form of a rhinoceros head. The man's burnt skull was devoid of hair but I could just make out a crumpled mass of stringy material near the forehead; the remains of the man's hat. His mouth was open full and wide and gray smoke emanated from it like a chimney. The brick walk underneath the corpse was unstained. Strange.

Carruthers coughed once then pulled a black leather object from his coat pocket, it cracked when he opened it. "I've got the man's billfold, Holmes," he said. "Found it in the bushes over there. Our victim's identity is-"

Holmes held up his hand. "No need to tell me, Commissioner," he said rather confidently. "It's Guardian Thomas Ramey. On the judicial bench for thirty years. I knew him well."

"But how-?"

"The head of his walking stick," Holmes answered as he stood up. "No one else in England has one like it. Is the billfold empty?"

"No. There's forty-two pounds cash inside."

"Then the motive wasn't robbery."

"The evidence seems to dictate so. I just don't understand it, Mr Holmes, Ramey was such a good man,"

Commissioner Carruthers said sadly, putting the wallet back into his coat pocket.

"Yes, he was," Holmes said, rubbing his chin. Then his glance fell upon the other constables searching the area. "What else have you found?"

"Three very strange, very small metal objects, dispersed in a wide pattern on the walk. I've left them where we found them, as you always instruct."

Carruthers led us to each of the metal objects. Each looked like melted ingots of silver, no larger than a match head. Holmes investigated them with the same vigor he investigated the corpse, only this time he brought out a handheld magnifying glass. Then he stood up, went over to the black, bloated corpse and looked into its mouth.

"I say, Holmes," Commissioner Carruthers began. "It looks as if someone who doesn't appreciate English justice and knew who Ramey was, accosted him, knocked him out, poured lamp oil over him and set him alight. Gruesome and abhorrent! What's this country coming to when a man can't stroll in a park peacefully? I couldn't even begin to think of how to find the perpetrator of such a crime, that's why I called you in."

"I'm glad you did, Commissioner," Holmes said. "And those shoes? Did you or your men disturb them?"

"No, we left them just as we found them."

Holmes nodded, stood in quiet thought for a moment, looked up into the sky then at the canopy of willows and oaks that towered above us. Why he was so interested in what was above us confused me. It seemed proper that everything he needed to solve the murder was below us, at our feet.

"Are you all right, Holmes?" Carruthers asked after a moment. "Do you know who the murderer is?"

Holmes' large brown glare came down out of the overcast sky then focused on Commissioner Carruthers. "Yes, I should think I know who the murderer is and she's a cunning, powerful force with no regard for reason or purpose. She kills at random and there's nothing we can do about it."

"*She?*" Carruthers and I exclaimed at the same time.

"Yes…*she*," Holmes answered boldly. "*She* struck Guardian Ramey while on his daily walk to work at the Royal Courts of Justice, with such force *she* knocked him out of his shoes, his billfold from his pocket and jarred the metal fillings from his teeth."

"Fillings?" Carruthers asked.

"Yes, Commissioner. That's what those small silver ingots on the ground are."

"Bloody hell!" Carruthers cursed. "The force it would take to knock a man's fillings from his teeth is almost immeasurable."

"I agree with you, Commissioner," Holmes said.

"But why would *she* splash him with lamp oil and burn him up like that?"

"*She* didn't splash him with lamp oil and burn him up, Commissioner."

"*She* didn't? But I can see Guardian Ramey laying there with my own eyes, black as a lump of coal-"

"Yes, Commissioner, but *she* didn't use lamp oil, *she* used a lightning bolt. Your murderer is Mother Nature."

THE CASE OF THE MARBLE GHOST

CHAPTER ONE: THE CLIENT INTERVIEW

"My wife has gone missing, Holmes, and I'm afraid I'm to blame," said our client, the illustrious Mr Timmons P. Walsh, ex-British Ambassador to Spain. He was a well-dressed, portly, older gentleman with thinning gray hair swept over to the right side, covering a patch of baldness that was glaringly obvious even without concentrating on it. He had a bulbous nose that hung like a door knocker over a full, bushy gray mustache. A pair of small, catlike eyes were bloodshot from attempts to halt the flow of tears. The thick fingers of his right hand held a nearly empty glass of whiskey as he sat stoically on a couch that seemed too small for him.

Holmes and I, for a change, were conducting the first client interview in the private study of Walsh's overlarge mansion on Gower Street in London as his fame would alert the daily rags if he were seen visiting us at our rather humble and exposed Baker Street address. Our search for his missing wife would have to be a secret affair if we were to successfully solve the case.

Holmes, pipe in his mouth, legs crossed, leaned forward in his chair then took the pipe out of his mouth. "Why do you blame yourself, Ambassador?" he asked.

"It…it was I who pushed her to get the damn thing done," Walsh answered, his eyelids blinked incessantly while he spoke. He looked up at Holmes and must have noticed my partner's inquisitive glare. "Do forgive me, Mr Holmes. Let me start at the beginning," he said, put the glass on a nearby side table and rose up from the couch. He went over towards the hearth, blazing wildly on this chilly November night, stopped, then pointed up at a portrait that hung above the mantle. A gloriously young and beautiful woman stared back at me from the canvas - brown eyes, tender mouth, long shining strands of ebony hair fell down around her shoulders, an ethereal glow emanated from her face as if filled with its own light.

"Your wife, I presume?" Holmes asked.

"Yes," the old man replied. With great effort, he tried to keep his eyes averted from the painting, as if looking at it caused him severe pain. "Eliza. I met her in Spain five years ago while I completed my ambassadorial tour for the Queen. She was the daughter of a wine merchant, very well-to-do," he stared at us a moment, noticing both our inquisitive glares this time. "I know what you're thinking, gentlemen…I'm an old, short, fat, ugly, comfortable man with only my own fortune to offer her, but she loved me truly just the same. As you can see, her beauty is unique in its intensity, unmatched anywhere in the world. I've seen men walk obliviously under the hooves of oncoming horses as they watched her cross a street. But, I tell you honestly, this portrait doesn't capture a scintilla of what her true beauty was like in real life. The first time I saw Eliza, standing under the shade of the balcony of her father's wine café one late summer's day, I noticed a warm, bright white light emanating from her and it was then I realized why a flower petal attracts a bee. In awe of the amazing beauty coming from both the inside and outside of Eliza, I was caught by her, at that very instant, forever. Apparently, and I don't understand it either, she'd felt the same for me and, gratefully expunging a lifetime of bachelorhood, I married her a month later." Walsh stopped again, looked down at the floor, clearly upset at the memory he'd just recalled, then he went over, picked up the glass and finished it dry. "We were happy, I tell you. My life had never been so pleasing, but being a practical man, as most men are, I knew that the ravages of time would someday destroy this angelic beauty of hers. It would be a sin to let that happen. It had to be preserved somehow, that's why I had that portrait commissioned by Britain's preeminent oil painter, Gerald Langley. He'd painted the Queen's portrait so his references were impeccable. Eliza protested at first but did as I had asked out of deference to me. She had not one bone of self-awareness or conceit inside of her so sitting for the portrait was a terrible ordeal for her and when it was finally finished, she refused to look at it, even after I had it hung up there above the mantle for the whole world to see. But as the days went on, it became obvious that Langley hadn't captured that essence…that spellbinding, ghostly light of her beauty. It was then that I contacted Master George Benford."

"I must admit, Ambassador, I'm not familiar with that name," Holmes said.

"What? Well, you should be, Mr Holmes," Walsh said irritably. "He's Britain's greatest sculptor. His bronze castings and marble works line the Mall outside of Buckingham Palace; Cornwallis, Horatio Nelson, The Duke of Wellington, and on and on. He's of such skill it is thought that he can capture the living soul of his subjects within the very medium he works. I thought, perhaps, he could do the same for my Eliza."

"Did she submit to this also, to please you?" I asked.

"Yes, of course," there was a note of regret in his voice. "Even though Eliza disapproved of it, she understood my mindset. So, this past spring, and at great expense to me, she began her sittings with Master Benford. I would take her in the hansom but Benford would only let me enter the studio when we first arrived. When he began working, it was made clear to me that I wasn't welcome. Like most artists of his talent and eccentricity, he demanded to work in private. So, I would sit outside in the hansom for three, sometimes four hours every day. I considered it a further price I had to pay if I was to get what I wanted. And Eliza, night after night, would come out from the studio, her mood melancholy, her mouth closed. This dour mood continued on at home, affecting every aspect of our private life."

"Did you suspect any tom-foolery between them?" Holmes asked.

Walsh frowned and his cheeks grew red in embarrassment. "You wouldn't ask that question if you knew Eliza, Mr Holmes," he said.

"Perhaps not, but it's been my experience that even the saintliest of people have their moments of weakness."

Walsh nodded. "You are quite correct in that supposition, but the answer is no. If I had suspected that, I would have forbidden her to go and shot the man."

"Quite extreme and very illegal, Ambassador," Holmes instructed. "Were you ever allowed to see the progress made on the sculpture?"

Walsh shook his head and poured himself another drink. "Not at first," he answered, took a quick swallow, then continued. "Every time I went into the studio Benford had an old, dusty blanket covering it. All I could discern was that it was a thin, vertical shaft of white marble, exactly as tall as Eliza was. Finally, after a fortnight I reminded him of the great expense I had incurred due to his commission and that as a client, I was entitled to see what he'd completed so far. After my tirade Benford relented and threw the blanket off."

For some reason Walsh stopped his story. His gaze danced away from us and fell upon the floor as Holmes and I waited patiently for him to continue.

"Forgive me, gentlemen," he muttered then took another drink. "This is very hard for me to admit. You see, he…he'd completed everything above her navel-"

"Her navel?" Holmes repeated, but both of us knew where this was going.

Walsh's whole face flashed undeniably deep red this time. "Yes, Mr Holmes. Her navel. Imagine my shock when Benford threw that blanket off, revealing my wife sculpted naked from the navel up, and it was clear what her hands were going to cover when he finally got down to that point. Eliza, seeing my reaction, fainted straight into my arms. I was enraged, if I hadn't been holding Eliza, I would have strangled Benford right then. To submit my wife to such base, erotic indignities…well…I was dumbfounded!" He slammed the glass back down on to the side table, struggled to compose himself a moment. "Then I looked up into the face he'd carved from the living rock…it was Eliza, her eyes were closed as if she was sleeping…but it was her! The softness, the light, the warmth, the beauty, the detail…Benford had successfully captured her essence in the marble, preserved it forever. It was miraculous. Against my strongest instincts, I let him continue… to bring the work to its proper completion, but I could no longer, in good conscience, be the one to bring Eliza to his studio any longer. The guilt at what I'd done, what I was putting her through was too much. Instead, I hired a cab to come collect her every morning at ten and bring her home at one in the afternoon."

This information perked Holmes up. "A cab, you say?" he asked.

"Yes. From Central London Cab Services," Walsh replied. "I requested the same driver pick her up every day, limiting the number of people who had insight about what my wife was doing. If it got out, the resulting scandal would ruin my reputation. The driver's name is Norman Bean."

"How well do you know this man?" Holmes asked.

"Not well at all. The only time I spoke to him was when I paid the fare in the afternoon after he dropped her off. He was simple-witted but seemed a nice enough man."

"Tell me about your wife's disappearance."

Walsh took a deep, loud breath then sat down on the couch again. "Six days ago, on the twenty-seventh of October, I sent Eliza off in the cab, just like every other day. I haven't seen her since. When the cab didn't arrive home in the afternoon, I contacted Scotland Yard immediately. They questioned the cab driver whom said he'd waited for her at Benford's studio for twenty minutes before going in, that was when Benford told him she'd left an hour before. Apparently she'd said it was such a nice day for late October she wanted to walk home."

"Did she walk often, Ambassador?"

"Never. She didn't feel safe enough in London to walk about on her own. What's troubling is that the distance from here to Stamford Street where Benford's studio is located is over five miles, and that's across the Waterloo Bridge. She would never attempt that. I fear the worst, Mr Holmes."

"Did the Yard talk to Benford?"

"Yes. He gave them the same story he gave the cab driver. After that they performed a cursory search of his studio and the neighborhoods between here and Stamford Street, but police resources being what they are nowadays…well, they turned up nothing, which leaves me in a state of limbo concerning my wife's fate. I'm positively frantic, Mr Holmes, so yesterday Detective Inspector Lestrade suggested I contact you. He said you're most capable at things like this."

"The Inspector flatters me," Holmes said without a hint of humbleness. "I think you've given me enough to get started, Ambassador. We'll be in touch. Thank you for your time. We'll let ourselves out."

"Thank you, Mr Holmes. If you need anything to facilitate your investigation, don't hesitate to call on me."

Holmes and I left the Ambassador sitting on his couch nursing another glass of whiskey. When we settled into the cab Holmes was silent in thought.

"Well," I began, breaking the uncomfortable silence. "At least we came away with two good suspects, the cab driver and the sculptor. We're doing better than usual."

"Three, Doctor Watson," Holmes retorted.

"What's that?" I asked, not quite catching his meaning.

"We have three good suspects, Watson," Holmes explained. "Didn't you notice that the Ambassador constantly referred to his wife in the third person?"

CHAPTER TWO: INTERVIEW WITH THE CAB DRIVER

Holmes, being a notorious late riser, didn't disappoint me the next day. Up at nine-thirty, he dressed quickly then we sat down and ate a hearty sausage and chip breakfast that Mrs. Hudson was good enough to prepare for us. Afterwards, armed with walking sticks, we took a cab to the offices of London Central Cab Services on Shaftesbury Avenue, found the manager then Holmes introduced himself. The manager knew of him and agreed to cooperate fully. Holmes asked him where we could find Norman Bean. The manager informed us that since Bean had lost a lucrative account recently, he'd been forced to work two shifts to make up for the discrepancy, so he was still out and about running the streets of London taking fares, even after working all night. He could be anywhere. The manager gave us Bean's cab number, 1930, then we left on foot.

"There must be dozens of cabs flitting all over London, Holmes," I offered. "How in blazes are we going to find Bean's?"

"By using logic, my dear Watson," Holmes replied cryptically. We started off heading northeast on Shaftesbury

Avenue then south on Charing Cross Road. Holmes seemed to know where he was going so I followed him quietly. It was the kind of delightfully mild, sunny morning that made foot travel bearable. On our left appeared Covent Garden, a grand sized public park always filled with people because the Covent Garden Market resided there. Trafalgar Square was further down at the end of the road and I could see the high, dark pillar of Nelson's Column in the distance. The glass fronts of countless businesses stared back at me from both sides of the road; a tailor, a shoe shop, a candy emporium, a cigar shoppe, etcetera. When we reached Strand, we turned northeast again, following it for some time until we reached the London Transport Museum. Outside the red brick façade sat a long row of black cabs, their burdens standing patient, blinders on, ready to transport fares. I'd never seen such a conglomeration of cabs gathered in one area before but kept my inquisitiveness to myself, knowing the answer would come from Holmes soon enough.

Holmes slowly inspected each cab as we passed by, each had a driver sitting out front holding leather reins in their fists, each stared at us as if we were the Queen of England, some even tipped their hats to us, hoping their geniality would secure a fare from us. They looked such a downtrodden, desperate lot I felt almost guilty at not hiring them in bulk. Then we came upon a cab, the only cab in the line, mind you, that was absent a driver out front. Closer inspection revealed the number on the cab to be 1930.

"Ah, here we are, Watson," Holmes said pleasantly. "Our mission is complete."

"And so it is," I agreed in amazement. "Tell me, Holmes, how did you know Bean would be here?"

"What time is it?" Holmes asked.

I pulled at the chain of my pocket watch and read the hands on the face. "Eleven twenty-two," I replied.

"The calm before the noontime storm," Holmes mused. "We are very near the center of London, look around you."

I did so and saw that we were surrounded on both sides of the street by banks, accountant's offices, barrister's offices, and high-end retailers.

"The heart of the business district, Watson, approaching lunch hour. Over the years I've noticed that cabbies gather here at this time every day, waiting to grab fares from those of the higher class breaking for lunch. In less than an hour there will be so much chaos here it will seem as if the entire street has been set on fire. Drivers incur more income during this one single hour than they do the rest of the day, so it was natural to assume Bean would be here."

I was not aware of this and I would definitely remember it for future reference. "But where is Bean himself?" I asked, pointing to the empty driver's seat.

"Remember, the manager told us he'd been working all night, pulling a double shift," Holmes answered. "You'll find that he's inside the compartment napping. Wake him up, my friend, and let's expedite this interview quickly."

I went over to the door and could hear the unmistakable rumblings of snoring coming from inside. I knocked on the window of the cab briskly, three times. I must have startled him because the whole cab compartment throttled to-and fro as if floating freely on harsh seas.

"'Oo th' bloody 'ell is it?" a suspicious voice rang out.

"My name is Watson," I replied. "I'm here with consulting detective Sherlock Holmes. We have some questions concerning the disappearance of –"

The compartment agitated again then I heard a long squeak followed by the slam of the door on the opposite side. Next, there were two hurried footsteps, a deep thud, a man's grunt. I realized Bean had been trying to make an escape by using the other door. This confirmed his guilt in my mind; why should he run if he wasn't guilty of anything? I called out for Holmes, looked behind me and discovered the great consulting detective was gone.

"I'm over here, Watson," my friend's voice echoed from the other side of the cab compartment. As I hurried around the back, I noticed that the other drivers were ignoring what was going on, wisely realizing that it wasn't any of their business.

When I reached Holmes, he was standing next to the cab with his walking stick held like a club in his hand. He'd cleverly predicted the man's escape attempt. Bean sat on the ground rubbing the top of his head with both hands.

"You didn't 'aff to 'it me so 'ard, sir," he complained.

"Up on your feet, Bean," Holmes said. "And explain why you ran."

Keeping one hand on his tender head, Bean used the other one to grab on to Holmes' outstretched hand, then stood up, a little wobbly though. He looked at Holmes then began: "I was scared, is all, sir. In recent days I been 'arrassed by police about a killin' I know nothin' about. An' then, respectfully, sir, but I don't know you from Adam an' you want to question me about it too. You could be th' killer for all I know."

"I never said anything about a killing," I protested. "I said 'disappearance.' Why do you think the woman you'd been driving has been murdered?"

"When a woman disappears in London, sir, it usually means murder."

"Sound logic, Bean," Holmes agreed. "Tell me about that day, the twenty-seventh of October, starting from when you collected Mrs Walsh at her residence."

"Well, sir, it be about ten in th' mornin', same time as every other day. The Ambassador escorted Mrs Walsh down th' stairs, 'elped 'er up into th' compartment, bid me good morning then went back inside."

"Did the Ambassador seem different that day? Angry? Sad?"

"No. 'E was more than regular, sir."

"Did you notice anything suspicious during the drive to Master Benford's studio?"

"Nothin', sir, other than that it was a bright an' cheerful day that day."

"What about when you dropped her off at Master Benford's studio?"

"No. Nothin', sir…wait! There *was* somethin' odd, now that I think about it. Master Benford actually came out of th' studio an' 'elped th' lady out of th' compartment."

"That's unusual?" I asked.

"It is for Master Benford, sir," Bean answered. "In all th' times I brought th' lady over there, 'e never came out. She always went in alone. And stranger still, sir, 'e seemed to be rushin' her inside, 'ad his hand on her back an' was pushin' her."

"Are you sure?"

"That's what I'll testify to, if I 'aff to, sir."

"What did you do after you dropped Mrs Walsh off? Did you come here?" Holmes asked.

"No, sir, didn't 'aff to at th' time. Th' Ambassador paid me real well, tipped even better. Some days I'd just drive round, catch short, local fares if I could. Other days I'd land a pub, 'av a few drinks until I 'ad to collect th' lady again. That day I picked up some fares an' with it bein' such a nice day, I drove through Covent Garden, watched people an' enjoyed th' weather. Nothin' special."

"And when you attempted to collect Mrs Walsh that afternoon, what happened then?"

"Well, she wasn't waitin' for me outside like she usually did, so I waited for damn near twenty minutes before I decided to go in an' see what was takin' 'er so long. Found Master Benford washin' 'is arms and 'ands in the sink. 'E was scrubbin' an' scrubbin' with a wire brush, but it didn't seem to be workin'. There was white stuff clingin' to 'im like paint. Then he saw me standin' there watchin' 'im an' 'e wasn't 'appy about it. Called me a few choice words, trespasser bein' one o' them, before I could get it out that I was there to pick up Mrs Walsh. That changed his tune right quick, he became all nicey-nicey, told me th' lady 'ad left an hour before, on foot. 'E even tried to shake my 'and but 'e still 'ad that white stuff on his 'ands an' I wouldn't do it. Took me a moment to realize 'e'd been laying concrete. Saw the fresh surface outside th' rear studio doors, leadin' to th' back yard."

"A patio?"

"Yes, sir. Small one, longer than it was wide. 'E did a terrible job of laying it, didn't seem to fit th' space properly. It was nice and perfectly flat, though, an' whiter than any concrete I ever saw before."

Holmes stared at the man, a look of intense concentration on his face. "Did you tell this to Scotland Yard, Bean?"

Bean shook his head. “No. Didn’t seem important at th’ time, sir, they were more interested in targetin’ me as a criminal so I was too busy defending meself.”

“My good man,” Holmes began. “If I pay you triple your fare, would you kindly take us across the river and to Master Benford’s studio as quickly as you can?”

CHAPTER THREE:
INTERVIEW WITH MASTER BENFORD

On the way to Master Benford's studio, we stopped at 4 Whitehall Place, the familiar location of Scotland Yard, and Holmes informed Detective Inspector Lestrade that he'd planned to interview the sculptor concerning the disappearance of Mrs Walsh. He requested Lestrade come with us, along with two constables armed with hearty sledgehammers and shovels. Inspector Lestrade didn't blink an eye at my friend's request as Holmes had proven his infallibility so many times in the past.

We arrived at Master Benford's spacious studio at high noon and caught him taking his lunch at the big oak table in his dining room. I don't know what Holmes had in mind but he ordered the two constables to stay outside until he called for them. I could tell immediately that Master Benford, a handsome, tall, muscular, older gentleman with thick, fuzzy black eyebrows and hair the color of an overcast London sky, was surprised and angered at our appearance in his home. He was still wearing his night clothes, slippers and a silver satin robe.

Holmes introduced himself and myself then apologized for the rude interruption of his midday meal. "But I'm sure you want to find Mrs Walsh as quickly as her husband does," Holmes said.

"Yes, of course, Mr Holmes," Master Benford said graciously, his dark countenance changed as quickly as the second hand's ticking position on a clock. "Please sit. Would you care for some tea?"

"Not right now, but thank you," Holmes said. "I wonder if you'd answer some questions I have concerning the day Mrs Walsh disappeared."

"I'll do what I can, Mr Holmes. Though, I'll have you know I've already been questioned by the Detective Inspector here, and quite thoroughly."

Holmes nodded. "When Mrs Walsh first arrived that day, how was her mood?"

"The same as always," Benford said. "Dour and melancholy. She hated coming here and sitting for me, even as I neared finishing the sculpture. I've never had an unwilling subject before and I must say it disturbed me. Made me wonder if there was something else she was truly unhappy about."

"Like what?"

Benford blinked his eyelids, took a deep breath, then answered. "Well, perhaps she's unhappy in her personal life, namely, with her husband."

“Did she ever say anything of that nature to you?”

Benford shook his head. “No, Mr Holmes, but for two decades many people have sat for me, have opened themselves to me, allowed me to bottle their souls in marble or bronze. I’ve come to know human nature intimately and can puzzle a person out quite quickly. Let’s take you for example…I can tell from your manner with me that you’re a man with few friends, you keep relationships on a professional, distant horizon yet you know the goings on in a new acquaintance’s mind just as intimately as if you’d known him all your life. And since you’re a civilian working by invitation of Scotland Yard, you must be a brilliant thinker or you wouldn’t be here questioning me. Am I close?”

I was draubled. In my mind, Benford had described Holmes perfectly.

This reverse interrogation didn’t seem to ruffle Holmes at all. “Close enough,” he said through a grin. “But let’s get back to the subject of Mrs Walsh. You said you were nearing the completion of her sculpture?”

Benford nodded. “Yes, Mr Holmes. In fact, I didn’t see the need for further sittings after the session on the twenty-seventh, that’s why I suggested we break early that day. I have but some minor alterations left and didn’t need her here any longer. Luckily, she hadn't gone missing until *after* that last session or the sculpture might never reach completion."

"That's a cold thing to say," I muttered in shock. "Mrs Walsh is missing and feared dead."

Benford looked at me with eyes that resembled dead black marbles. "I'm sorry if my attitude upsets you, Doctor Watson, but I'm an artist not a police inspector. I was commissioned to produce a piece of art, nothing more."

Before I could pursue this damnable subject, Holmes interrupted me. "May we see the piece of art in question, Master Benford?" he asked.

Benford's gaze returned to Holmes. "I'm afraid not. It's always been my policy never to show unfinished work to outsiders. Only the client, Ambassador Walsh in this case, has any right to see it."

"Ambassador Walsh is also a client of mine. I can assure you that, as a hired agent of his, I have his full permission and confidence to see the piece."

Benford reached forward, picked up his tea cup, took a sip, then placed it down on the plate with such care the porcelain made no noise. I was disliking this man more with each passing moment. Finally, he glanced at Detective Inspector Lestrade. "Is this true?" he asked.

"I referred Mr Holmes to Ambassador Walsh personally," Lestrade answered.

"Then, the matter is settled. Follow me, gentlemen."

***

Holmes, Lestrade and I followed Benford out of the dining room, past the parlour, across the foyer and through two large French doors leading to Master Benford's studio. Immediately upon entering the large, rectangular space, I was overwhelmed by the heavy odor of dirt and paint.

The floor consisted of white stained and very worn wood slats, I could tell it had been swept thoroughly very recently. There were tables all around jam packed with small clay and marble studies of the male and female bodies in different poses. Against the plastered wall to my right, or the north wall, were a row of life sized, marble sculptures of the common British man toiling in his every day labors; a sailor shoveling coal into an imaginary boiler, a chef preparing an imaginary meal and a stone mason wearing an apron, holding a brick in one hand and a trowel thick with mortar in the other. They were extremely realistic interpretations of their subjects and could, in my opinion, be readily displayed in any museum. Alongside those were several large, virgin blocks of square and rectangular marble underneath aged canvas sheets, waiting to be cut and formed.

We passed through a path made by the cluttered tables, through the center of the studio, going towards the far wall, or west wall, where a sink and the huge opened steel doors of a kiln resided in the corner, a pair of steel rails came out from the depths of the kiln, inside I saw a flat surfaced cart on steel wheels covered in what looked like piles of melted white clay. Next to the kiln was an unlit hearth with old, dented cans of paint collected about it. The entire wall beside the hearth was covered completely by the dusty tools of the sculptor's trade, hanging by nails and screws, so thick in some places I couldn't see the white plaster of the wall underneath. Benford had them labeled with wooden signs hung crookedly; *Violin Drills, Calipers, Chisels, Hammers, Mallets, Carving Sets, Riffler Rasps*. Some looked to me like the enlarged dental instruments of some giant's hellish dental office and were well used, worn to grotesque points and abstract angles. What their proper appliance was, I could only guess. Holmes seemed very interested in them, his gaze was long and narrowed in their direction as we walked through the room.

Against the south wall were marble sculptures of shapes resembling twisted, malleable things, tall and short, thick and wide, the capacity for my mind to describe them properly is beyond its limits. I was amazed, though, at how Benford could make something as hard and dead as marble seem rubbery and alive. Another double French door stood closed but present on that wall, outside I could see the new, flat, thin, misshapen patio the cabby had spoken about earlier that morning.

Benford led us to the southwestern corner of the studio where a sculpture stood by itself under a red paisley, silken sheet. This alone denoted the sculpture's specialness. Peeking out from the bottom of the sheet were a row of small, white toes, naked as a baby's. Without saying a word, he reached up, grabbed the sheet and pulled it off.

There she stood, Mrs Walsh in all her mesmerizing, naked beauty. She seemed to be sleeping while standing up, her skin was as smooth as glass, her proportions were perfectly executed. The details of her face, her mouth, nose and around her eyes were attempted with such skill, I half expected her to open her eyes and begin breathing. It was an amazingly realistic, breathtaking work. Not even the faint spidery veins of gray running through the entire surface took that realism away.

Holmes' voice awoke me from my deep admiration. "What's that, Master Benford?" he asked. He was pointing at a small, thumb-sized triangular pit centered in the area between

Mrs Walsh's breasts, right where her heart would be if she were a real person. The pit resembled an inverted three-sided pyramid, its sides perfectly smooth, its edges sharp and fresh. This was a detail Ambassador Walsh had left out during our first interview. I wondered why? Perhaps he'd been so taken with the face he'd missed it completely.

"An imperfection. That's one of those minor alterations I have to correct, Mr Holmes," Benford answered, his dark eyes were large and entranced on the sculpture's eyes as he spoke.

"Hmmm," Holmes murmured as he looked over the entire sculpture. "Stunning indeed, Master Benford. Ambassador Walsh was right, you have miraculously captured his wife's unique beauty. Your reputation is confirmed."

"Thank you, Mr Holmes," Benford said, still staring at the sculpture's face. His eyes were glassed over now. "May I cover her up? I don't want to risk any peripheral damage."

"Of course," Holmes said. As Benford draped the sheet over the sculpture, Holmes' gaze fell upon the patio outside. "New patio, Master Benford?"

At those words, Benford's entire body became like one of his sculptures, frozen in time. Holmes had struck a nerve, though I had no idea why. Then, after a nearly imperceptible moment, he removed his hands from the sheet and shared Holmes' gaze. "Why, yes, Mr Holmes," he said calmly. "Nice of you to notice. Laid it myself only a few days ago."

"It looks a very competent job. May I go out and see it?"

What a strange request coming from Holmes, I thought. Here we were trying to figure out where Mrs Walsh may have gone off to and he was impressed by a simple patio.

"I-I," Benford stammered. "Oh, all right, but it's nothing really. I'm not satisfied with it and plan on having a professional replace it."

Holmes grinned. I'd seen that grin many times before, when he was about to spring a trap. "Oh, come now, Master Benford," he began. "I couldn't have done a better job of it myself. Inspector, have a look with me, won't you?"

Lestrade shrugged dutifully, following Holmes' lead. Holmes opened the door and we all stepped outside to admire the patio. The yard was completely lined with a ten foot high wooden fence, blocking the view of every house surrounding it. There was a gate at the northeast corner of the house and countless piles of jagged, useless marble rubble sat all over the yard, very little grass showed through. We stood around the perimeter of the patio, quietly staring, as Holmes slowly went to and fro, inspecting every inch of it. I watched Benford watching Holmes, he'd caught a slight tremble and his face turned pale as his hair.

"As you can see it's nothing special, Mr Holmes," Benford said, his voice had suddenly acquired a soft vibrato.

"On the contrary, Master Benford," Holmes said. "It's a very special size…just large enough to cover a corpse!"

So that was what Holmes was after! Benford's eyes went so wide they nearly popped out of his skull. Lestrade quickly grabbed the sculptor's wrists, put cuffs on them then called out for his constables. They came through the rear gate immediately, sledgehammers and shovels in their hands.

Holmes turned to the artist. "You won't mind if we look under the rug, do you, Master Benford?"

"What-what's this all about?" Benford asked angrily, his face had regained some of its color.

"It's about the disappearance and murder of one Mrs Walsh," Holmes explained. "Whom you buried under this block of concrete to conceal your crime."

"Murder?" Benford repeated. "That's preposterous! I have no reason to have killed her! Her husband has paid my commission fully!"

As the constables tore into the concrete with their sledgehammers, throwing dust and cement chips into the air, Holmes responded to Benford's claim. "It wasn't about the money, Benford. You've got enough of that to last a hundred lifetimes. It was about love."

"Love? Are you crazy, man?"

"You can't deny it, Benford," Holmes said. "You had motive, means and opportunity. Mrs Walsh was a remarkably beautiful woman, a blind man could see the way you looked at her sculpture a few minutes ago. Did you kill her because she refused to return your sentiment? Did she threaten to tell her husband about your feelings? Spill it!"

"I have nothing more to say, Mr Holmes," Benford spat defiantly.

"Wise policy, Benford," Holmes agreed. "Save it for the jury."

The concrete broke up rather easily, in most places it was only a few inches thick. The constables threw the larger pieces on top of one of the nearby piles of rubble then, when the area was completely cleared of concrete, they began digging into the soft, moist black soil. Down into the dirt they went, huffing and puffing, for many minutes until they had gone so deep they couldn't climb out without help.

It appeared that there was nothing “under the rug,” as Holmes had put it. Mrs Walsh’s corpse was not to be found there.

CHAPTER FOUR: HOLMES IN ERROR?

Holmes appeared frustrated and despondent in the cab on the way back to Baker Street. I knew it would be my death if I said anything so we rode home in silence. A few blocks from Baker Street, Holmes ordered the driver to stop.

He turned his mercurial head and looked me right in the eyes. "I apologize for any humiliation I've brought upon you today, my friend," he said.

"No one is perfect, Holmes," I said. "Don't worry about me. I don't care about myself one whit."

"That's awfully good of you," he murmured then sat back and closed his eyes. "The thing is, I know Benford did it. Every arrow of the compass comes back to him, I just haven't all the facts yet."

"What are you going to do?"

Holmes thought about it a moment then sat up again. "I'm going to figure it out, my dear Watson. Don't wait up for me." And with that he was up and out of the cab, hurrying south down New Bond Street. There was a confidence in his steps I found encouraging.

***

When I got back to Baker Street, Mrs Hudson noticed my dark mood and made me a nice, warm, chicken breast dinner with onion soup. She ate with me at the dining table Holmes and I usually shared and did her best to cheer me up with shallow conversation, but unfortunately, my mood had decided to remain stubborn. And it became even more so when a telegram arrived from Master Benford, demanding Holmes and Detective Inspector Lestrade come to his studio the next morning at nine and give him a public apology for what was almost his false arrest, defamation of character and for destroying his newly laid patio. Every crime reporter from every city newspaper had also been invited, which meant that the cat had been let out of the bag concerning the disappearance of Ambassador Walsh's wife. The missive continued on, stating that the Ambassador himself was invited to collect the sculpture of his missing wife at the same time, thereby ensuring even more publicity for Benford. With the great sympathy the newspapers would surely generate for him among the commonwealth, Benford would have new commissions lined up for years to come.

Clever bastard, this suspicious artist!

After Mrs. Hudson left, I lit a cigar and ruminated in my chair in front of the fire with a glass of brandy. Then I pulled out a hardbound leather book from off the shelf, a series of short dramas of horror and intrigue by *Sir Arthur Conan Doyle*, and read until the heaviness of sleep fell over me like a ten tonne weight.

When I awoke the next morning I was still in my chair. The sun had just cleared the dark rooftops of the city and delivered another predictably gray November day through the open curtains of the parlour window. I heard a crinkling noise and found Holmes standing near the now extinct fire reading the telegram.

"Oh! Where have you been, Holmes?" I grumbled through a yawn.

Without removing his eyes from the telegram, he answered: "Educating myself, Watson."

"About what?"

"Many, many things."

"I see you found Benford's invitation," I said as I pushed myself out of the chair. "Are you game?"

Holmes forced the telegram into his coat pocket and faced me. "I wouldn't miss it for the world, my friend," he said.

***

When we arrived at Master Benford's studio promptly at nine, chaos was the order of the day. Reporters and curious onlookers spilled out of Benford's front door like confused ants on an ant hill.

"Are you sure you're up to this, Holmes?" I asked as we sat in the cab, watching them through the window.

"Of course, Watson," he replied. "I will do this with dignity and as much humility I can raise."

This certainly didn't sound like the Holmes I'd grown to know and respect over the past three years. He opened the door and I followed him out into the melee. Questions were thrown at Holmes as we cut our way through the crowd: *What evidence made you suspect Master Benford? Where do you think you first went wrong about Master Benford? Will you work with Scotland Yard again? Is this your first failure?* And on and on. Holmes didn't answer a single query, he just stoically charged his way up the stairs, into the foyer and through the doors of Benford's studio.

There were so many people in the studio their body heat negated the need for a lit hearth. The din of countless voices, the odor of sweat, cigarette breath and cheap cologne swirled around in the air in thick swatches of invisible fog. Thankfully, more to show the reporters what Holmes and Lestrade had done to his patio rather than bring any fresh air into the room, Benford had the rear French doors open. A gentle, cool breeze equaled things up nicely.

We found Benford, Ambassador Walsh and Detective Inspector Lestrade standing in the corner in front of Mrs Walsh's sculpture, which was still covered by that red paisley sheet. Detective Inspector Lestrade stared at us with a low grimace, his eyes set under the deep shadows of his dark eyebrows. I noticed he gave Holmes a quick nod, though his facial expression remained the same. The Ambassador extended a hand to Holmes and they shook.

"I'm sorry about all of this, Ambassador," Holmes greeted.

"So am I, Mr Holmes," Walsh said then gazed teary eyed upon the covered statue. "I am not going to take the sculpture home. I can't bear it. The humiliation of this publicity circus turns my stomach and is against everything I was hoping to accomplish. The sculpture has become nothing more than a ghostly reminder of my wife, cold and unreal…incapable of receiving or giving love. If only Eliza were here, in the flesh, I would destroy it with my own hands…make amends for everything I'd done to her."

“I would help you with that, Ambassador Walsh,” Holmes said then Benford, noticing that we were all here, raised his hands and quieted everyone down.

“Yesterday,” Benford began. “Scotland Yard, represented by Detective Inspector Lestrade and aided by consulting detective Mr Sherlock Holmes…” he motioned towards them as he spoke their names, “came into my home and grossly accused me of murdering my client’s, Ambassador Walsh’s, lovely wife, Eliza. With wanton disregard for the law, they ordered constables armed with sledgehammers and shovels to destroy a patio I had just laid and then dug up my yard in a misguided attempt at finding her body.” He pointed at the pile of dirt and the deep hole left just outside the French doors. The sledge hammers and shovels had also been left behind, because Benford had been so insistent on getting everyone off his property as quickly as possible, and were leaned up against the inside studio wall next to the opened French doors as evidence to reporters of Scotland Yard’s much too enthusiastic attempt at investigation. Very cleverly staged!

Detective Inspector Lestrade’s face turned pale, his mouth and chin squeezed hard in embarrassment. Holmes watched Benford, betraying no emotion other than keen, calm interest, his hands clasped confidently behind his back.

"I tell you all truthfully," Benford continued. "That I had nothing to do with Mrs Walsh's disappearance. I was hired by the good Ambassador to capture his wife in marble. She would sit for me and I would sculpt. I have had no other relationship with her other than that. As proof of this, I will reveal to you the work in question and would ask the Ambassador to collect it for transport home after these proceedings."

Ambassador Walsh shook his head defiantly. "I've told you already, Master Benford, I will not take it home. It has no meaning for me until my wife is found, dead or alive! And I will not stand here while you sully her memory by showing the sculpture in this public proceeding. It is a deeply personal work fit for my eyes only! You should all be ashamed of yourselves!"

"I disagree, Ambassador," Benford retorted. "It is an object of such beauty, such skill, in the realm of the classical Greek marble works of old, that it should be appreciated by the people of the entire world. I am not ashamed of what I've done! In fact, I'm proud of it! It is my greatest work!" With that, Benford reached over, grabbed the sheet and pulled it off with a flourish. A wave of awe-inspired, stunned *oooohs* and *aaaahs* swept over the reporters, not a single one had pencil to paper. I noticed that Benford hadn't corrected the triangular pit that hung in the marble between the breasts, but everything else was perfect beyond imagination. The reveal had happened so quickly that the Ambassador hadn't had time to fight his way through the crowd. His face squeezed into a tight ball of red anger as they all ogled his wife's nude form.

Holmes quickly grabbed the Ambassador's forearm and leaned in to his ear. "It is in your best interest to stay for the entirety, Ambassador," Holmes murmured. "We should know where your wife is very shortly."

The Ambassador's mouth fell open in shock as he let Holmes return him to his place in front of the statue.

"Detective Inspector!" one of the reporters blurted out. "Is that the lady you are searching for?"

"It is," Lestrade replied. "If any of you has seen Mrs Walsh, contact Scotland Yard immediately." *Now* the pencils started to tear up paper, it sounded as if a thousand rats were scratching at the baseboard of a wall.

"As a public figure and a proven honest businessman, I've gathered all of you here today to publicly demand vindication of my good name in the form of a sincere apology from Scotland Yard and Mr Sherlock Holmes," Benford went on. “And monetary restitution to rebuild the patio I spent an entire day laying.”

All eyes fell upon Detective Inspector Lestrade and Holmes.

Holmes turned towards Lestrade. “Allow me to go first, Inspector,” he said then stepped forward to address the reporters. “I apologize to Master Benford. It was my erroneous deductions that led to Scotland Yard tearing up his yard with these.” Holmes pointed to the sledgehammers and shovels leaning against the wall. With the grace of a ballet dancer, he slid over, grabbed a sledgehammer and held it horizontally in both hands. Then he just as gracefully slid back into his place to the right of the statue. “I never should have ordered the good constables of Scotland Yard to use these on his patio. It was my error and my error alone. Scotland Yard should not be held in further contempt for the results of my actions. You see, I should have told them to use it on this sculpture!” With that exclamation, Holmes brought the iron head of the sledgehammer backwards then forward, sending it into the upper spine of Master Benford’s greatest work with a deafening grunt!

CHAPTER FIVE: HOLMES REDEEMED?

Screams and shouts exploded from every corner of the studio as the sculpture rocked forward from the momentum of the sledgehammer's head, nearly falling forward. The blow sounded like two stone blocks crashing together. Dust sprayed into the air but nothing resembling slivers of stone or marble followed. Instead, the area where Holmes hit the sculpture seemed to cave in, absorb the blow. Jagged cracks slithered across the once perfect surface of Mrs Walsh's carved face.

As Holmes brought the iron head back for another try, Benford, enraged beyond all reason, shouted "NO!" at the top of his register and rushed Holmes, but Detective Inspector Lestrade caught him and secured his wrists with cuffs, just as he did the day before. Holmes' second blow to the upper spine was the capper. The stone from the shoulders up exploded, large continents of oddly shaped debris spun away in quick arcs, splattering on the ground at the reporters' feet.

The shock, the intense horror, of what was revealed to everyone in that moment stilled those in the studio to silence. Sprouting out of the remnants of what was left of the stone was Mrs Walsh's actual head, neck and shoulders. Her long black hair had been straightened and disappeared down her back and into the confines of whatever made up the shell she was encased in. Her chin was resting low, her eyes were closed, preserved in the exact pose the finished external skin of the sculpture had shown. Her true skin was devoid of color, covered in a layer of white dust. I'd seen some horrifying things in my days fighting in Afghanistan, but this was worse than anything I could ever recall.

"My Eliza!" Ambassador Walsh cried and fell on to his knees, grasping desperately at the legs of the statue. Again, none of the reporters were putting pen to paper as they were completely involved in the drama unfolding on the stage before them.

Holmes knelt down, picked up one of those jagged pieces of debris that had flown off after the second blow, then he stood up again. "Concrete," he said as he held it out for everyone to see. "Cleverly painted and coated to resemble marble."

"My God, Holmes!" I ejaculated in disbelief. "The atrocity of it…h-how did you know?"

"It was my failure at the patio that set me on the right path, my friend," Holmes answered. "I noticed as the constables were breaking it up that it had been set far too thin for practical use, only a few inches thick in some places, it would crack once the first person stepped on it. So I asked myself, why should Master Benford, an artist who works primarily in stone and obsessed with details, do a half-buggered job of laying a simple slab of concrete? The obvious answer was that it was runoff."

"Runoff?" I asked.

"Yes, Watson…runoff; extra concrete left over from a previous job. Then I asked myself, what was that previous job? Benford had no other areas of construction going on in the house or the studio. That was when I remembered the flat surfaced cart sitting in the kiln and how it was completely covered in what resembled piles of dried white clay. It occurred to me that it was most likely dried concrete."

With everyone watching, I hurried to the kiln, reached in and pulled the cart out. A handful of reporters helped me and we inspected Holmes' theory. "You're right, Holmes," I said. "It's not clay or anything related to a kiln firing process. It's most definitely set and dried concrete. But what's the point of it?"

"That, my friend, is where Benford lay Mrs Walsh down and skillfully but hurriedly covered her in a layer of extra fine concrete, quick drying on the morning of October twenty-seventh."

Looking down at it, Holmes' deduction made perfect sense. I, along with the handful of reporters stepped away from the cart in horror.

"You see, Watson," Holmes continued. "After I left you in the cab yesterday, I went to various local store fronts that carried construction materials, asking managers if they'd sold any materials to Master Benford, who is quite a well-known celebrity in this city. They would surely remember him. But every time I asked, the answer came up in the negative. Then I happened upon an institution only a few blocks from here named The Greater London Masonry Emporium. The manager, a Mr Springly Reese, quickly remembered that Master Benford had been in on the twenty-fourth of October, three days before Mrs Walsh had gone missing, and purchased three forty pound bags of extra fine, fast drying concrete. All one has to do is add water and apply." Holmes reached into his inside coat pocket, pulled out a small slip of yellow paper then held it up over his head. "And here is the receipt, dated and signed by Master Benford himself."

The pencils were scratching away again, much more furiously this time.

“But three forty pound bags of concrete,” I surmised aloud. “That seems too much to cover a body of Mrs Walsh’s petite size.”

“Correct, Watson,” Holmes agreed, nodding as he gave the slip to Detective Inspector Lestrade. “Master Benford had made a crucial mistake. You see, he’d done this dastardly deed before, three times to be exact, but on men of husky build and above average height and he mistakenly used the same calculations of material he’d used on those three men on Mrs Walsh, finding, to his utter dismay, that he’d had too much concrete left over after completing Mrs Walsh’s encasement. Knowing that he didn’t have much time to hide his error, as Scotland Yard was sure to be placing a visit upon him concerning his latest client’s disappearance, he cleverly used the extra concrete to make a patio, thinking no one would suspect a thing and if they did, they would find nothing underneath, as I had proved only too eagerly.”

“But these three men you speak of,” I asked. “Where are they?”

Holmes pointed to the north wall and everyone looked in that direction. “Over there,” he said. “Those sculptures of the sailor, the chef and the stone mason. Those were Benford’s practice pieces. I’m sure when Detective Inspector Lestrade gets around to them later, he'll find three men encased inside a layer of the same kind of concrete that Mrs Walsh is currently encased in." Holmes faced Lestrade. "They'll be transients with no name or history. Completely devoid of identification of any kind and untraceable."

Lestrade nodded in understanding.

With everyone's attention focusing on the three statues, no one had noticed that the Ambassador had removed himself from the floor and was staring at the pale, lifeless corpse of his wife. "But how did he kill her, Mr Holmes?" he asked, his voice trembling with deep felt emotion. "Did he put his filthy hands around her neck and strangle her?"

Holmes shook his head. "No, Ambassador, he stabbed her with a riffler, right through the heart."

"That explains the triangular pit in her chest," I said, pointing to the mark still on Mrs Walsh's chest, where the concrete hadn't broken off yet.

"Correct again, Watson," Holmes agreed. "The same pit Benford called an 'imperfection' that needed 'minor alteration.' It's the clue that actually confirmed my deductions as to what had happened. I remembered that during the first interview with the Ambassador, he didn't mention this mark, and he surely would have if he had seen it. This meant that this statue was not the original carved from the first block of marble that the Ambassador had seen, but it was a second later version. This pit is actually the fatal stab wound, carefully preserved by Benford."

"Preserved?" I asked incredulously. "Why would he want to preserve something of that nature."

"Because, my friend, whenever Benford sees it, it allows him to relive that exact moment in time when he murdered Mrs Walsh, something most sociopaths cherish. It's like the gold locket you carry with you that reminds you of your mother, Watson. It brings back a clear, distinct, warm memory of her in your mind whenever you see it. That's why he never altered it. Benford knew that the good Ambassador here would never take something of this flagrantly erotic nature home, he could never show it to people and it would always remind him of his missing wife. Master Benford correctly assumed, therefore, that he would remain in possession of the statue forever."

"But why?" I asked.

"It's the one thing I was right about yesterday, Watson," Holmes explained. "Benford's motivation for killing Mrs Walsh was unrequited love. Isn't that so, Master Benford?"

Benford just stared at Holmes, his eyes dark and soulless.

"Day after day, over the weeks and months, as Mrs Walsh sat for him, her intense beauty wore him down. Soon, he'd realized he'd fallen in love with her and then it developed in his mind that she might possibly love him back. Because, he rationalized, a woman of her beauty couldn't possibly love a man of the Ambassador's plain and meager façade. Yet, here Benford was…tall, successful, handsome, famous and has had personal audience with the Queen and many other official dignitaries. He was clearly the better choice. But this fantasy turned out to be erroneous, didn't it, Benford?"

Again, no reaction from the sculptor.

"Of course it did. Benford hadn't counted on the fact that Mrs Walsh may actually have been in love with her husband. So, realizing that he was nearing completion of the actual marble statue of her likeness and that he wouldn't be holding audience with her any longer, Benford decided to confess his true feelings to her on the morning of the twenty-seventh. And it went badly. But he'd planned for this scenario, he'd practiced and perfected, over the years, his method of skillfully covering his victims over with fine-grained, quick drying concrete, painting it to look just like marble. The crime would be so unbelievable and carried off with such skill, no one would figure out what happened to Mrs Walsh. So, Benford and Mrs Walsh argued and in the heat of the moment, he took a riffler off the wall and plunged it into her heart, the very thing he desired more than anything else in the world, to possess."

"But what's a riffler, Mr Holmes?" the Ambassador asked, his eyes red with tears.

"Good question, Ambassador. Being somewhat ignorant in the detailed production of many forms of art, I didn't know what a riffler was either. After I visited those construction suppliers, I went to London University and interviewed the artist in residence, Mr Orville Stringdon. He educated me on every tool and carving method a sculptor of marble would use. I found out that a riffler is a small or medium sized file-like tool used for shaping and smoothing stone, distinguished by size and the shape of its file heads, like those hanging on the wall over here." Holmes confidently went over to the west wall and stood in front of the section marked "RIFFLERS" on a large wooden plate. "As you all can see," he said. "All the tools on this wall are covered by a thin layer of white marble dust. All of them except one…Number Seven." He pointed at the object in question, its two, pointed metallic heads indeed sparkled in the sunlight coming through the six skylights above. The other rifflers were dull and unremarkable. Holmes reached out and pulled the tool from its perch on the wall. Then he held it out for everyone to see in his two palms, as if he was catching rainwater. "Why does this one, and none of the others, seem brand new? Because it has been recently cleaned of Mrs Walsh's blood. Let me prove it to you." Holmes went over to Mrs Walsh, took the riffler in one hand, and slowly, carefully slid the tip of one end into the triangular pit between her breasts.

"It fits perfectly!" a reporter gasped and an excited buzz spread through the crowd.

Holmes handed the riffler to Detective Inspector Lestrade then addressed the throng of reporters. "I have proven to all of you Master Benford's motive for the murder of Mrs Walsh, his unique method and that he had clear opportunity. You may write it up as you will, but now, I implore you to exit the premises and give the good Ambassador proper privacy for the display of his grief."

***

Holmes was right about the three statues against the north wall. Once their concrete shells had been broken apart, the desiccated skin, muscle and bones of three anonymous victims were revealed. These, along with Master Benford, the receipt from The Greater London Masonry Emporium, the riffler and the carefully preserved concrete section of the wound in Mrs Walsh's chest, were taken by Detective Inspector Lestrade and a group of constables to Scotland Yard in preparation for Master Benford's trial, which promised to be the highlight of the year.

After everyone left and silence fell over the studio, Holmes and I helped the Ambassador lay his wife's corpse down on the wooden floor and removed it completely from her concrete shell. Then we covered her under that red paisley sheet so the Ambassador could pay his last respects in some measure of dignity. I said a short prayer, aloud, then Holmes told the two Scotland Yard morgue workers waiting outside in their wagon to come in with a gurney and collect Mrs Walsh.

"I do have one last question, Mr Holmes," the Ambassador said.

"I will answer it if I can, Ambassador."

"Where is the original piece of marble Benford was working on before he murdered Eliza? I saw it myself on many occasions."

Holmes looked away a moment, through the now closed rear French doors in the south wall. Then he answered. "Are you sure you want to know that, Ambassador?"

Holmes' tone sounded dire. I couldn't think of anything worse than what I had just witnessed in the studio a half hour before but apparently my brilliant friend knew better. The Ambassador took a deep, violent swallow then nodded.

"Follow me then, Ambassador," Holmes said and led us through those French doors, into the back yard. Scarred with a deep hole dug by Scotland Yard constables the day before and dotted with countless piles of marble debris Benford had been amassing for decades, it was an eerie feeling navigating through the chaotic maze in the calm of the early November mid-morning sun. The carelessly tossed away remnants of Benford's entire life lay in the rubble represented back there and now I couldn't help but think how his life had ultimately imitated his art in this way.

Holmes stopped in front of a rubble pile near the back fence. The shards here were bright white and large, as if dumped there recently. "I noticed this yesterday as we were leaving," Holmes said. He pointed and upon closer inspection I saw Mrs Walsh's face peeking through a break between two huge crumbled blocks of marble. She seemed to be sleeping peacefully, even though her graceful nose had been chipped off and the perfect lines of her face had been interrupted by deep scratches.

The Ambassador leaned over, moved the two stone blocks away with his hands, revealing what was left of his wife's ethereal beauty. Everything under her shoulders had been broken and shattered, ruined forever. To me it was as if Mrs Walsh had been murdered twice.

"Benford couldn't have two versions of your wife's statue hanging around. How could he explain that? So he had to destroy the original. I'm very sorry, Ambassador," Holmes said, the heartbreak in his voice was clearly apparent.

But the Ambassador smiled. "No, no! Can you see it still, Mr Holmes; in the stone…her essence…the ghost of her beauty? It's all there if you look hard enough," he said.

He was right. Even though I'd never met her and even though the marble had been irreparably damaged, there was something special, something alive in the cold hardness of his wife's imperfect image. In silence, Holmes and I helped the Ambassador carry the still lovely ghost of his wife to his hansom.

THE PREDICTABILITY PROBLEM

On the morning of the twenty-fifth of June, while we were having our mid-morning tea in the parlour of our flat on 221b Baker Street, Holmes received a missive from a youngish messenger in the employment of the British Government.

"It's from my dear older brother Mycroft," Holmes said as he focused on the note. "He requires our presence at the Diogenes Club forthright."

The Diogenes Club, the most anti-social gentlemen's club in London, founded by Mycroft a few years ago, was a rather controversial institution. No talking or excess noise of any kind was permitted, the committee that governed the club was very strict in adherence to this policy…three offences and your membership was rescinded. I thought it a strange request, then, that Mycroft ask that we meet him there.

Obediently, we followed the messenger down the stairs and into a waiting government hansom, which took us directly to the seven story hotel on Millbank Street, across from the British Parliament building, where the top floor was entirely reserved for the club itself. The messenger silently led us into the heart of the club, a large quiet space with forest green carpeting and dark cherry-wood veneered walls. On the north wall was a line of bookshelves stuffed to the limit with leather-faced volumes, giving the room the definite air of a library for the elite. Three windows framed by green velvet curtains broke up the monotony of the outside wall, giving an impressive view of the parliament building across the street. Two dozen deeply cushioned, high-backed chairs were scattered all over the room, just far enough apart from each other that it prohibited any temptation of even whispered conversation. Each chair had its own side table and lamp, all but five of them were filled with stodgy gentlemen in dark suits reading the dailies and smoking cigars. It was so quiet as we walked in that I could hear the tendon in by bad left knee stretching and recoiling in protest.

We weaved through the maze of chairs, the men in them ignoring us completely, until we came to a chair directly in front of a window that was turned away from us. I saw the top of a man's head sitting motionless beyond the seat's high backing, the hair was brown and thin. The messenger went around, made himself seen, nodded at the man, then at us, then he left us alone.

As Holmes and I positioned ourselves in front of the man, the man carefully, quietly, folded up his newspaper and crossed his legs. He was young but older than Holmes, a little heavier in build, with a high forehead in the early stages of revealing itself completely. But I could clearly see the family resemblance. Holmes and Mycroft stared at each other for many moments and I began to suspect that perhaps they were having a kind of psychic conversation. I wondered what they were saying and felt distinctly out of the loop. Suddenly, Mycroft's eyes flashed upon me, his gaze eyed me up and down then fell upon Holmes again. All this theatre seemed ridiculous to me until Holmes, in a bout of impatience, began tapping on the table, not with his fingernail but with the fleshy tip of his finger. I recognized it immediately as Morse Code, knowing it well from my training while serving in the British colonial force in India.

What's this all about? Holmes tapped.

Mycroft smiled, reached over and replied in the same: *Your government needs you.*

I don't work for the government.

Mycroft nodded then tapped: *Consider yourself drafted then.*

Out of the question! Holmes replied but with such passion the sound of it nearly rose to eviction level. Holmes was never one to be forced into doing something.

Mycroft put his hands up, as if to calm his brother down, then waved for us to follow him. Once we were out in the reception area, the doors to the club securely closed behind us, Mycroft turned and faced Holmes.

"Let me explain," he said. "Have you ever heard of Jules Verne?"

Holmes stood there for a moment, trying to recall the name, then he turned to me and I shrugged in complete ignorance. "I'm afraid not, Mycroft," he finally answered.

"That's incredible," Mycroft said, shaking his head. "He's the most famous French writer living. *20,000 Leagues Under the Sea*, *Journey to the Center of the Earth*, *Mysterious Island* and a whole line of other novels of adventure and science, the worldwide public is absolutely crazy for them."

"Why would that be important to me?" Holmes asked.

"Well, many of his books predict what life in the future may be like. In some circles he's considered a prophet of sorts and this concerns the British Government?"

"Why? He's but a writer of fiction, that's what they do. One can't take what he imagines seriously."

"Yes," Mycroft agreed. "But lately he's made certain predictions about the future of the British Empire and they don't sound fantastic. In fact, they're downright frightening."

"Even so, what does that have to do with me?" Holmes asked.

"As a member of a covert government brain trust, I've talked with the man, heard the details of his thesis and now share the government's concern. I fear what he says may come to fruition. I would like you to interview him, see what your impression is. He's expecting you."

"He's here?"

"Down on the third floor," Mycroft answered through a nod as he led us to the elevator. "He's here in London looking for a publisher to translate his books into English. He's sailing back to France in a few days, so we don't have much time. Can I count on you?"

Holmes stared down at the floor, rubbed his chin while in deep thought and as the elevator doors parted, he nodded. "Yes. I think I would like to have a try at debunking his theories, and perhaps restore peace to our government's troubled mind in the process," he said and we entered the elevator.

***

The man who met us in his hotel room was anything but a green-skinned, one-eyed, hunchbacked, pimple-nosed, witch wearing black robes holding a crystal ball over a boiling cauldron full of children. He was a tall, distinguished looking man in a black suit with silvering hair, mustache and beard. His handshake was strong and confident and when he led us into the room, there was a round table with an opened bottle of red wine and four glasses on top.

"Would you care for a nip?" Verne asked in French.

Fluent in French, Holmes and I declined the author's offer and everyone took their seats around the table.

"I'm very pleased to finally meet you, Mr Holmes," Verne opened cordially. "Thanks to Doctor Watson's articles in the papers I'm quite familiar with your adventures."

"Thank you, Mr Verne," Holmes said. "I do apologize if I can't say the same about you. My profession doesn't leave much time for light reading."

"I understand fully, Mr Holmes. No offense taken."

"My brother, Mycroft, explains that in your fiction, you've made a series of predictions and some of them disturb him. On what basis do you make these prophecies?"

"Like you, Mr Holmes, I use clues and deduction to arrive at a conclusion, except that the clues I use are found in the overall evolution of human history. I take the past and extrapolate forward accordingly. It's quite an obvious process when you think about it," Verne said. "For example, using this method I can predict that, in the future, horse drawn carriages will move on their own, without horses or steam engines. And from that I can predict that the horseless carriage will someday take to the skies, transporting people from town to town and perhaps even across the ocean - and some of these flying cars will be able to house hundreds of people…there will be great clouds of them moving in the skies day and night. In fact, flying will someday be such a common, everyday occurrence that people on the ground won't even acknowledge their existence as they pass by overhead."

"Incredible!" I ejaculated. "Horseless carriages that move by themselves? Flying across the seas? By what magical power source will this be possible?"

"There will be a new form of liquid energy discovered that will allow the horseless vehicle to travel hundreds if not thousands of miles on a single tank, perhaps that energy source will be liquid hydrogen or concentrated petroleum. I can extrapolate this theme even further and say that one day men will travel to and live on the Moon."

"By means of horseless carriage?" Holmes asked.

"No," replied Verne. "An elevator will one day be constructed that will be connected from the Earth to the Moon. It will take only three days to travel the distance between the two objects."

"Men living on the Moon? Bah!" I exclaimed.

"Nevertheless, Doctor, I predict that it will happen."

"Let's change the subject," I suggested. "In a personal interest, what advances do you see occurring in medicine?"

"Good question, Doctor," Verne said. "It's a subject I've spent much time and energy thinking about as I currently suffer with diabetes. I expect that medicine will eventually allow surgeons to replace every part of the human body, like a landowner replaces bad posts in a fence. This will permit men to live to many hundreds of years old. Which, of course, leads to the possibility of human overpopulation of the earth and the depletion of our natural resources, such as water and forests."

"That's sound like both a positive yet grim future we're heading for," Holmes said.

"There's always good with the bad, sir. The ancient story of life on this planet."

"Which includes war, Mr Verne," Holmes said. "What are your thoughts on that?"

"I can imagine that war will eventually be fought completely by machines," Verne answered. "Giant cylindrical missiles, controlled by men hundreds of miles from the front by means of electronic signals, will be capable of destroying objectives miles in diameter with their unbelievable energy. This will mean that the current laws of war will no longer be honored, civilians will be considered viable targets, and only in this way will victory be secured."

"Terrifying," I said. "And despicable."

"Which leads us to the reason why this meeting has been arranged," Mycroft interrupted. "The future of the British Empire."

At this moment, Jules Verne felt it proper that he should pour himself a glass of wine. After a long, careful hoist, he placed the empty glass down and began. "I'm afraid, gentlemen, that the British Empire will be extinct within three or four decades."

This comment, delivered with such a severe calmness and coolness, by a Frenchman whom I knew no better than Adam, brought my temper to a boil. "Poppycock!" I shouted and slammed a fist down on to the table, surprising everyone. "I have been wounded in service of my country so that she shall exist forever…I find it hard to believe that she shall disappear within my lifetime. The next thing you'll say is that there will be invisible men stalking the Earth, or beings from another planet invading our cities or that someone will invent a time machine!"

Verne sat there, unmoved and emotionless at my outburst. "I predict none of those things, Doctor," the author said. "They are simply too fantastic and not based on the historical method I adhere to."

"Tell me, Mr Verne," Holmes said. "What leads you to make such a startling prediction?"

"The fact that every empire that has ruled the Earth has eventually collapsed," Verne answered. "The Egyptians, Persians, Greeks, Romans, Spanish. What makes the British Empire any different? Already there is rebellion among certain British Colonial sects in India and West Africa. Within a few decades, this rebellion will so tax the Empire's treasury that she will have to consider constricting, to protect her very existence. In essence, the British Empire has spread itself too thin and doesn't possess the monetary nor the human resources to maintain itself."

"You've gone too far, man!" I erupted again.

"Calm yourself, Watson," Holmes demanded. He was taking this insult a little too well for my tastes. "Mr Verne," he began. "If you are correct and she should fall, which country shall succeed the British Empire?"

Without skipping a breath, Verne said: "The United States."

"What?" I asked. "That young, rebellious bastard son of our empire?"

"You underestimate them, Doctor," Verne said. "They have the natural resources and will have the military strength to lead the world through the twentieth century."

"Unbelievable!" was all I could utter, my temper had paralyzed my tongue. Nothing the man had said tonight was credible in any reality I lived in.

"Well, I think we've taken up too much of your time, Mr Verne," Mycroft said. "I apologize if the passions in this room became too heated."

"I understand completely, sir," Verne said. "I would feel the same if someone had talked about my beloved France the way I talked about Britain."

We got up from our chairs and shook the author's hand. I sincerely apologized for my outburst then we left. In the elevator going down to the first floor, Mycroft turned to Holmes. "So, what's your opinion?" he asked.

"Complete drivel, dear brother," Holmes answered. "You'd be wasting your time if you took anything this Mr Verne said seriously."

"Others in the government agree with you," Mycroft said. "But I'm not so sure. Something in my gut tells me to believe him and to prepare certain contingencies to circumvent the alleged coming catastrophe."

“Mycroft,” Holmes argued. “Flying vehicles, elevators to the Moon, two hundred year-old men, the United States ruling the world…and you want to believe in the fall of the British Empire after all that?”

Mycroft thought about it a moment then nodded. “I suppose you’re right. When one thinks about it, I guess it does sound unbelievable.”

“Good man,” Holmes said. “Come, we’ll get some tea and forget all the nonsense we’ve just heard. I’m sure the British Empire is safe and sound for centuries to come.”

BANE OF THE BLACK BRIGAND

I

Holmes had just captured my queen with his knight when we heard the voices coming from downstairs, 221a, Mrs Hudson's flat.

At first they were just mumbles and I found it odd that Mrs Hudson was keeping company with another person, especially a man, at this late an hour on a Friday night. Then the mumbles became hurried, angry declarations – words like *No! Stop!* and *Mine!* could be clearly discerned. Mrs Hudson's voice rose and fell with the man's voice and when I glanced up at Holmes, I saw that he was clearly troubled by what he was hearing. His concentration on the game had been irrevocably broken as he stared at our front door, listening, my queen dangling in his two fingertips like a piece of fish bait suspended in time.

In the three years we'd been living there, I'd never heard Mrs Hudson's voice in such a state of agitation or fear. I must say, it brought out the protective inkling in my make-up; I wanted to go straight down and make sure she was all right. Then the banging started, the floor trembled under our shoes, the portraits on the walls vibrated, nearly falling off. When Mrs Hudson let out a sudden scream, Holmes dropped my queen down on to the table and stood up. I joined him immediately, but we stood silently like pawns on a chess board, listening with concern. There was a loud, deep thump, followed a short time later by a violent bang that shook the whole flat, then there was a long silence.

"Holmes," I said, my voice trembling. "I think we should-"

"Right, Watson," he interrupted, grabbing his loaded Webley from a nearby book shelf. "And now!"

We sprang for the door, opened it then raced down the seventeen steps it took to reach Mrs Hudson's darkened parlour. No one was in there but a small fire flickered in the hearth against the far wall near the couch. From the kitchen came the familiar clicking of the water pump and a series of fierce hisses, alerting us to a presence in there. Holmes, his pistol pointed forward, led the way.

The gas lights overhead were on full, nearly blinding me as we rushed in. We found Mrs Hudson standing in front of the sink basin, her gray hair, usually pulled back in a tight bun, was loosened and hanging down around her aged face like weary cobwebs. Her face was flushed of color and matted with a layer of perspiration, the glare of her eyes never left their focus on what she was furiously washing in the basin with a rag; a long, wood handled carving knife covered in a thick, red viscose material. The water in the basin was stained pink but was becoming darker the more she splashed and scrubbed.

But the true gobsmacker was on the kitchen floor near the opened inner door to the mud room, just beyond Mrs Hudson - a copper haired man lay there on his back, his arms and legs spread, a circular red stain drenched the white of his shirt over his gut. He looked to be in his late thirties, maybe early forties. Without thinking I rushed over and knelt beside the man, found no pulse. He had a wide, stout face but a long, slender ridged nose, his mouth was agape as if frozen in shock, his green eyes stared blankly up at the ceiling.

“Mrs Hudson?” Holmes asked, his voice sounding as bewildered as I felt. “Who in blazes is that man? What happened here?”

She ignored him and continued to scrub the blade free of blood.

II

While Holmes comforted a deeply disorientated Mrs Hudson on the couch in the parlour, I watched as Detective Inspector Lestrade and his contingent of constables searched the flat and the copper haired murder victim for clues.

The man had a billfold stuffed so thickly with five, ten and twenty pound notes that he had it secured with a rubber band, but there was no form of identification inside. He wore the clothes of a man in leisure, freshly pressed green suit coat and pants, freshly shined shoes, a black tie. The white dress shirt that had been pierced by the knife was made of the highest quantity thread count Egyptian cotton, the most expensive of its kind found in a London clothier. Since the victim lay in front of the inner door to the mud room, I deduced he'd come into the flat through the rear outer door of the mud room as Holmes and I hadn't heard the front door open with its distinctive squeak that night, and we had been sitting playing our game in silence for many hours so we would have heard it clearly. The rear outer door of the mud room was in pristine condition, knob, jam and lock intact, so Mrs Hudson had let the man in, which meant she knew him – but she wasn't talking.

She just looked at Holmes and Lestrade with a determined stare as they asked her their questions.

"You can trust that I will eventually get to the bottom of this, Mrs Hudson," Holmes stated. "You might as well answer my questions now, make it easier on everyone."

But again, her answer was a stare that rivalled the coldest, emotionless mannequin standing in a store window.

"What are you hiding, Mrs Hudson?" Lestrade pleaded, frustration scratching his usually smooth voice. "Who are you protecting?"

Those were the right questions, but answers were not going to be had. Her eyes stared forward, her mouth was clamped down tight, jaw jutted forward.

Lestrade threw his hands up. "I'm sorry but you leave me no choice, Mrs Hudson," he said impatiently, waving a constable over to collect her. "Maybe you'll talk down at Scotland Yard."

The constable stood next to her and waited while she sat there, obviously contemplating what her next move should be. Then her blank stare turned defiant. She nodded, stood up, held her arm out, allowing the constable to take it and lead her outside.

After she'd been extricated from the parlour, Holmes got up off the couch and approached Lestrade.

"Be gentle with her, Detective Inspector," he said. "I gather there's a good, decent reason she's not cooperating and as I said, I will get to the bottom of it. I just need some time."

"We'll treat her right and proper, Mr Holmes," Lestrade said. "But remember, you yourself caught her alone, standing over the dead body, washing off the evidence on the murder weapon. And I'll not be able to control a jury that hears that bit of evidence."

Holmes frowned then nodded. The three of us knew that a hangman's noose awaited Mrs Hudson should she be convicted.

Once Lestrade and the rest of his men left, Holmes stood near the closed front door, chin on his chest, arms crossed in severe thought. "We must help her, Watson," he said.

"Yes, of course," I agreed. "But she won't cooperate with us. We'll have to do it on our own, without her blessing."

"So be it, my friend."

"Well, what'll we do first?"

After a moment of introspection, Holmes finally replied: "The answers to what happened here tonight…who that man was, why he was murdered, are in this flat, Watson. We must turn it over with the instincts of a bloodhound."

"But Lastrade and his men have already-"

"Yes, I know, but they are not Mrs Hudson's friends, Watson. Come, help me."

III

Holmes and I filtered through the parlour first, and through the closet underneath the stairs leading up to our flat; found nothing out of the ordinary except an old black fur coat I thought very much out of Mrs Hudson's price range. Holmes stored the fact of its existence into his memory and we continued. Feeling queasy about doing it myself, Holmes decided to go through Mrs Hudson's bedroom while I searched the kitchen.

I had no idea what to look for but did it anyway, knowing the life of Mrs Hudson depended on what we found in the flat. Holmes assured me that I'd know a vital clue when I came to it. But I came across nothing of note.

Feeling overwhelmed by emotion for our good landlord's looming fate, I sat down at one of the chairs around the dining table and ran my fingers through my sodden hair. How such a thing like this could happen to Mrs Hudson was beyond me. If I hadn't seen it for myself, I wouldn't have believed it. The visage of Mrs Hudson standing at that sink basin, calmly cleaning the blood off a kitchen knife like an experienced killer kept replaying through my mind in fast, blurry patches. Nothing made sense. It was sheer madness Holmes and I were up against!

Finally, exhausted mentally, I rubbed my eyes free of the horrible memory then saw a small red stain on the white tile of the kitchen floor where the copper haired man's corpse had lain an hour before. There it was, positive, full color proof that my memory hadn't been faulty. What I'd witnessed earlier had actually happened. I could come to no other conclusion except that frail, innocent, elderly Mrs Hudson had murdered the man, the only question was why?

I noticed the inner door to the unlit mud room remained open, revealing a small, shadowy eight by eight space with a rear door leading to the alley behind the flat. It had been the only room the constables from Scotland Yard hadn't searched. I sympathized with them but decided it would be best to at least perform a cursory search, that would pacify Holmes, I thought. As I pushed myself up and out of the chair, my peripheral vision caught sight of something in the dark glass of the kitchen window near the inner door. When I flashed my full attention upon it, I saw the ghostly image of a man's angry face staring back at me, white as a sheet with a wide face but a long, slender ridged nose and copper-colored hair.

The sudden shock of the man staring back at me through the window startled me so terribly that I jumped and backed into the wall, knocking a candle sconce to the floor. When I gathered myself up enough, I looked back at the window and saw that the face had disappeared. Had I troubled myself so much with the memory of Mrs Hudson's plight that I imagined the thing? My instincts knew better.

"Holmes!" I cried and in rushed the consulting detective.

"What happened?" he asked, glancing quickly at the shattered sconce on the floor. "I heard a crash!"

I pointed at the window, my hand shaking. "I-I saw a man…there…staring at me through the glass!"

Holmes' sharp gaze dashed to the window. "A man? Are you sure?" he asked.

I nodded stupidly.

"Calm yourself, Doctor! What did he look like?"

I ripped my attention from the empty window and looked at Holmes, "As God is my witness," I began. "It was the man found murdered here on Mrs Hudson's kitchen floor!"

IV

Holmes found some brandy in a cabinet above the sink basin and poured me a glass. Sitting again at the table I took the glass and swallowed it down briskly. The warmth of it soothed my incessant shuddering.

"Feel better?" he asked.

"Yes, very much. Thank you."

He sat down at a chair across from me. "Now, tell me again what you saw," he requested.

I took a deep breath, for this had been the third time he'd asked such a favor from me. "I saw the face of the dead man on the floor standing there, staring at me through the window," I replied. "I-I know it sounds mad but the hair, the nose, the green eyes, it was him, I tell you!"

Holmes sat back in the chair, staring at me but his glare was dreamy and unfocused, he was thinking. "I believe you, Watson," he finally said.

"You-you do?"

"Yes. It confirms a suspicion I've had since we first came down those stairs."

"What suspicion?" I asked.

“That there was another person down here with Mrs Hudson and the victim,” Holmes replied confidently. “A third person…the actual murderer.”

“A third person?” I echoed. Now I was wondering which one of us was going mad.

“Yes, Watson. Remember the thump and the bang we heard while listening upstairs?”

I did remember it and nodded.

“It’s my suspicion that the thump was the dead man hitting the floor and the bang was the rear outer door of the mud room slamming shut.” I must have looked unconvinced because Holmes got up, “Here, let me prove it to you,” he said then went into the mud room, grabbed the door knob of the outer rear door and twisted it. “Listen closely as I slam the door.” He pulled the door back then thrust it forward as hard as he could, into the jam. The resulting bang I heard next exactly resembled the sound I’d heard earlier.

Holmes came back into the kitchen. “You see? It couldn’t have been the dead man and it doesn’t make sense for Mrs Hudson to have killed the man and, with bloody knife in hand, rush over to the back door, open it, slam it closed, then go back to the basin and start cleaning the blade. No…there was most definitely a third person down here with them tonight and he escaped through that door."

"But the man I saw resembled the victim," I reminded him.

Holmes rubbed his chin. "Yes, it may have been a projection illuminated by your mind or it may have been something else, something I'm still not convinced of yet but it explains how Mrs Hudson knew the two men and why she's protecting the murderer."

"But why would the murderer come back to the murder scene, risk getting caught?"

"There's something here he wants," Holmes answered as he glanced around the room. "Perhaps something he left behind. He figured that after Mrs Hudson was taken away by the police the flat would be abandoned, it would be safe enough to come back and steal it away. But he saw you through the window and fled when you saw him. That's why, Watson, we need to scour this flat from top to bottom."

"Well, I've searched in here and found nothing," I interjected. "I was going to start in the mud room when I saw the face in the glass."

"Then I'll help you, my friend. Come, the work will ease your nerves."

Holmes took an oil lamp from off the countertop near the sink basin and lit it, then I followed him into the mud room. The walls were painted yellow and the only window was the small square one cut into the door. A pair of leather boots, their soles thick with dried, crusty soil, lay on their sides near the door. The floor was made of weathered wooden slats, covered with a large, dirty brown rug patterned with green flowers. There wasn't much, in my estimation, to see in there but Holmes forged on, swishing the flickering lamp around the room, illuminating every corner and crevice with soft yellow light. Then he came to the rug and stopped with a violent double take. It was something I'd seen him do whenever he discovered a well hidden clue. He knelt down, placed the lamp on the wood floor next to the rug and leaned forward, a magnifying glass suddenly in his left hand. With the fingertips of his right hand, he skimmed the flowered pattern of the border.

"Ah! What have we here, my dear Watson?" he asked rhetorically.

V

The light from the oil lamp exposed a long, thin inverted shadow on one side, spanning the entire length of the rug – there was seam of some kind in the floor underneath.

With great vigor, Holmes grabbed the end of the rug and threw it back, revealing a trap door built into the floor. A squarish, shallow indentation was built into on one end of it and a thick loop of lightly frayed rope lay inside the indentation, perfect for lifting the door up.

"What in blazes?" I asked.

"There seems to be another level to Mrs Hudson's flat, my friend," Holmes said. "Shall we explore it?"

I felt a little uneasy at delving into our landlady's personal business and hesitated to answer, trying to think the morality of it through first.

"Watson," Holmes said. "I believe the answers to Mrs Hudson's problem are down there, should we ignore it and let her face the gallows or -?"

"I understand the situation, Holmes," I replied curtly. "It's just that whatever is down there she obviously wants kept secret and I'm afraid of what we may find out about her. It's none of our business."

"No, but our friend's well-being is," Holmes stated, reached down, grabbed the rope and pulled. The trap door came up easily on its hinges, revealing a wide row of stone and mortar steps leading down into an endless darkness. He carefully brought the door all the way back and laid it down on the floor, then he took up the oil lamp and stepped into the darkness of the vault. The odor of soil and must filled my nostrils, telling me that the vault below had been dug a long time ago.

I followed Holmes all the way down, a dozen steps in total, and when we reached the bottom his oil lamp exposed a sparse, rectangular room not much larger than the mud room above, with brick walls and a stone floor. There was a single wooden chair with a flattened gray cushion standing like a sentry in front of Holmes. Beyond that, against the west wall, was an altar-like cherry wood table with an unlit candle on top, but a single drawer and a small steel Mosler safe underneath. Hanging on the wall above the table was a painted portrait of a young, attractive red haired woman and a dashing, dark haired man. Both were wearing what resembled their Sunday finest; she in white, he in black. Holmes held the light forward as he stared at the portrait.

"Who are they?" I asked.

“Isn’t it obvious, Watson?” Holmes replied.

Taking a little more time I inspected the portrait more deeply, especially the woman, it was the eyes I recognized first. “Why, it’s Mrs Hudson, at a very young age!” I said in amazement. “How beautiful she was.”

“Yes,” Holmes agreed wistfully. “The slow crawl of age has a way of erasing beauty, in every woman, so that she is nearly unrecognizable later on.”

“That means the man next to her must be her long deceased husband.”

“Yes, the ever-present yet never discussed Mr Hudson,” Holmes said as he glanced around. “Judging by the worn cushion on the chair, she comes down here often, lights the candle and stares at the portrait, remembering. It appears she’s still grieving.”

“After all these years?”

“Grief is different for everyone, Watson. But you already know this.”

I nodded.

Holmes put the lamp on the table and opened the drawer. Inside was a rather large Holy Bible with a leather cover and gold embossed writing. He reached down, pulled it out and placed it on the table where I could see yellow slivers of loose, torn paper sticking out from the pages. I joined Holmes at the table and watched as he opened the Bible, coming across the first slip of paper, it was a newspaper article dating from 1832 and concerned the robbery of a government official while traveling on a forest road south of London during the night of July, 11th. The official, though unharmed, had been carrying notes in the amount of forty pounds intended for the purchase of a plot of land near the coast. The robber was dressed all in black, had a black scarf over his face, rode a large brown steed and used a pistol to intimidate his victim. Holmes turned to the next insert and found yet another article dated a few months later, about a brigand dressed all in black who had robbed a local business man of his payroll, again it had happened on a forest road at night.

"Why would Mrs Hudson preserve these articles?" I asked.

"Let's continue," Holmes answered and came to a third article, the editor by this point in March of 1833, had come up with a catchy name for the dastardly thief – *The Black Brigand.* The dozen or so articles that followed all referenced the Black Brigand who seemed more a ghost than a flesh and blood human criminal, escaping from every trap the authorities set for him. He had a penchant for disappearing without a trace into the darkness of the woods after his crime, not even the tracks of his mount could be followed. Meanwhile, as the years passed, the jewelry and coinage the mysterious thief had amassed was ever growing, well into the many thousands of pounds. Finally, Holmes came to the final article, dated August, 1842, detailing the shooting of the Black Brigand by the Sheriff of Walworth, who'd set a trap, pretending to be another government official transporting a chest filled with two pound coins to Her Majesty's Royal Navy. The bait was too tempting, though transparent in hindsight, as no government official would ever travel without Royal guard into the forest with a chest full of English mint. The display of the Black Brigand's body in London's Central Square set people's fears at ease, though the true identity of the thief had never been discovered. No one who'd seen the corpse, at least publicly, recognized it.

Holmes turned to the Book of Revelations and there he found an ancient envelope stained with yellowed dots. On it was scribbled *Last Will and Testament of George Anton Hudson of Bermondsey*. Perusal of the will showed that it was drawn up in June of 1842, two months before the death of the Black Brigand and executed in August of 1842 – it was clear to me from the carefully preserved articles and the execution of the will that the Black Brigand was Mrs Hudson's husband, George. The will stated Mrs. Martha Louise Hudson was the inheritor of a forty-three thousand pound fortune and was to allocate, in monthly installments, the sum of twenty-five pounds on the last Friday of every month to each of her twin sons, Ernest and Charles, a rich payout at the time. This was to go on until the death of Mrs Martha Louise Hudson, then what remained of the sum was to be distributed evenly among the sons.

"Twins?" I ejaculated. "Mrs Hudson is a mother? Why would she hide something like that from the world?"

"I'm sure it had to do with the fact that her husband was the Black Brigand and she didn't know about it until he was shot dead. If it came out that she had sons who were annually receiving the stolen booty pinched by the Black Brigand, She and her sons risked going to prison."

"But she knows she can trust us –"

"Everyone has their secrets, Watson, even you and I. Believe it or not, I'm as stupefied by this as you are," Holmes said. "But it confirms my earlier suspicion; that you'd seen the twin of the murdered man in the window, he was the third man in the flat tonight… the murderer. That's why Mrs Hudson isn't cooperating with Scotland Yard, she's protecting her only remaining son."

"It boggles the mind, Holmes!" I exclaimed. "Mrs Hudson married to the Black Brigand! I remember hearing stories about him from my parents as I was growing up. They used him as a sort of bogey man to scare me into staying in bed at night."

"And now, forty years later after his death, the bane of his ill-gotten gains have caused the predictable disintegration of his own family," Holmes stated.

"You think greed was the motive for the murder, then?"

"Indeed, Watson. What else could it be? That's why the brother returned to the flat tonight, to collect the rest of his inheritance then disappear, perhaps leave the country. The safe where the booty has been kept all these years is right there, at our feet, all we need to know is the combination."

"Surely you can break into it?"

"Of course, but that would diminish its use as bait."

"You mean to trap the murderer in the act when he returns?"

"Why not? It worked against his father, it should work against his son."

VI

Holmes went up, shut off the gas to the lamps in the kitchen then cleverly placed the rug over the trap door from underneath, while on the steps inside the vault, making the flat look abandoned, the trap door undiscovered.

Then we hid in the small space next to the steps, extinguished the oil lamp wick and waited in silence. Holmes had his pistol out and ready. He was betting that the man would return again that night, and he was right.

It wasn't an hour later when we heard the creak of the back door opening followed by footsteps thumping above our heads. Then the trap door flew open and the shadowed figure of a man came down the steps in a hurried, desperate gait, his right hand holding a lit lamp of his own high and forward. He stopped at the table, placed the lamp on top then knelt down, quickly spinning the dial on the Mosler's steel reinforced door. I could see from the glare of the lamp that he had copper colored hair.

There was a loud click and the man clapped his hands together in satisfaction. As he reached into the bowels of the safe, Holmes stepped out of the shadows of our hiding place, pistol pointed at the man. "Are you Charles or Ernest?" he said once we were close enough. Thinking quickly, I re-lit our lamp in case the man tried to pull a fast one and extinguish his to make an escape.

The man froze in place, his hands still plunged deeply inside the Mosler. "Who-who are you?" he asked.

"Friends of your mother's," Holmes said as he carefully stepped around so that he stood next to the table, facing the man. "Slowly pull your hands out of there and stand up, we have much to talk about. Do you have him, Watson?" Holmes bluffed, making the man think I had a pistol trained on him.

"Yes, Holmes," I said boldly, playing along.

The man did as Holmes ordered, then stood there with his hands up.

"Frisk him," Holmes said.

I did so, found nothing dangerous on his person.

"Sit down," Holmes ordered as he waved the pistol at the chair.

The man, hands still up, did as told.

"Well?" Holmes asked. "Which one are you?"

Visible beads of sweat were gathering on the man's brow, I was amazed at how closely he resembled his brother. "I'm Ernest," he said weakly, his green eyes were wide and intent upon my compatriot's figure.

“Ernest,” Holmes began. “I’m Sherlock Holmes, this is my friend Doctor John Watson. What kind of man is it that lets his mother take the fall for his own crime?”

“It’s not like that, Mr Holmes. I was going to send the Yard a letter, detailing the whole story once I was safely out of the country-“

“I don’t believe you,” Holmes interrupted. “Tell me what happened tonight that made you kill your own brother.”

Ernest took a long, hard swallow, then began talking. “Charles and I never got along. The only time we ever saw each other was when we’d meet in our mother’s kitchen to receive our monthly endowment. He’d been complaining recently that he needed more…he wanted mother to double his stipend, which was contrary to father’s wishes-“

“Do you know who your father was?” Holmes asked.

Ernest nodded. “Mother told us about it after he was killed. You must believe me when I say she knew nothing of his activities. Father kept everything hidden from all of us, we didn’t find out about the safe and what was in it until after the will was read. And even then it was hard for her to obey his instructions, knowing that our inheritance was collected under dubious circumstances. But we were destitute at the time. Father was an unskilled man, worked odd jobs wherever he could find them, barely kept food on the table for us. That's why he turned to crime, Mr Holmes…to support us. The only time I ever saw him spend any money was when he bought mother a coat she'd seen in a store window in London."

"A black fur coat, like the one upstairs in the closet?"

"That's the one, sir," Ernest said. "He brought it home for her a few days before he was killed but she never wore it. Ever. Charles talked about pawning it for cash all the time…how that angered mother so."

"I assume, after Charles demanded an increase in his endowment, an argument ensued."

"And nothing mother or I said to him could change his mind," Ernest answered, staring down at the floor. "I understood his argument, of course. We're both approaching fifty and, like they say, you can't take it with you. He wanted to live the good life before he died, waiters and dinner parties and such, but mother was against anything pretentious like that. She was afraid that, even after all this time, people would suspect where his money came from if he began showing it off. She was very ashamed of it, never took a single shilling from the safe for herself as far as I know. Always called it a curse upon our family."

“She was right,” Holmes said. “Tell me about the actual murder.”

“Charles threatened to tell everyone who father really was if she didn’t give him the increase, expose the one family secret above all others that would destroy all of us. Hell, even Charles and my existence was kept secret from everyone. I couldn’t let him do that to mother, I had to protect her…so we fought…during the altercation my hand fell upon a carving knife lying on the counter near the sink basin.” Ernest’s eyes began glistening with tears as he did his best to control his voice, avoiding a complete breakdown. “It-it all happened so fast, Mr Holmes. I didn’t even know I’d stabbed Charles until he fell to the floor and mother screamed. Realizing the horrible crime I’d committed, seeing the deep sadness and horror in my mother’s eyes, I panicked, dropped the knife and ran out of the flat. But I’d left without my part of the monthly stipend, I couldn’t leave the country without it, so I came back a little while later to take it all, hoping things had settled by then and the flat abandoned…that’s when I saw Doctor Watson in the kitchen…and he saw me.”

A long, terrible silence followed as Holmes and I stood there digesting what Ernest had told us. I couldn’t have felt more sympathy for Mrs Hudson, or more powerless to do anything about it.

"On your feet, Ernest," Holmes said. "We must take this story down to Scotland Yard and free your poor mother from your father's terrible curse. Watson, grab a container and secure the booty. It must be extricated from this house and given to the proper authorities. Only then will some form of peace fall over Mrs Hudson."

VII

After Ernest told his story to Detective Inspector Lestrade, Holmes pleaded for leniency in the charge against him, citing the terrible loss Mrs Hudson had already endured of one son. Convinced it was the right thing to do, Lestrade charged Ernest with the secondary crime of defensive manslaughter, which carried with it a maximum sentence of ten years in prison.

Holmes promised to testify on Ernest's behalf, this eased Mrs Hudson's mind considerably and in the hansom on the way back to 211a Baker Street, she held on to Holmes' hand, never letting it go, grateful that he'd given her a chance at a new life.

We never spoke of the incidents of that night again, nor of Mrs Hudson's marriage with the Black Brigand. One day, a month later, I heard hammering going on in down in 221a. When I asked Mrs Hudson about it, all she would tell me was that she'd finally put the past behind her.

Good for her.

THE LATE CONSTABLE AVERY

As I sit here in the sunny parlor of 221b Baker Street, taking my afternoon tea, I'm suddenly struck with the urge to tell you about a most interesting case my good friend, Sherlock Holmes, and I tackled together early on in our friendship. It was a rather unexpected affair.

The constables of Scotland Yard hold their annual benefit to raise funds for the *London Constables Retirement Fund* on the last Friday of every October and this particular year they'd asked Holmes to give a short speech about his recent, wildly successful partnerships with Scotland Yard. But getting Holmes to appear at any public function has always been comparative to putting a collar on a feral cat. His blade-sharp mind considered public appearances and speeches utter faff; pretentious strokes of the ego. It took a fortnight of prodding by me, thickly printed flattery from various editorial columnists of local news sheets and a personal request from Commissioner of Scotland Yard, Yancy Carruthers, to convince him to take a night off from his mental ruminations and violin practice.

As our cabriolet rode up to the marble stepped entrance of the London Central Event Hall on Belgrave Street, I asked

Holmes if he'd had his speech with him. He shot me a confident glare and tapped his fingertip to his temple. "It's all in here, Watson," he said.

"Quite, quite, of course," I agreed, sincerely embarrassed at my error. Holmes had the memory of a hundred pachyderms.

When we entered the event hall we found it full of formally dressed constables and their wives. A five piece brass band played *"Oh, Tallulah"* on a large stage at the rear of the hall but I could barely hear them over the din of countless voices and jovial laughter. Immediately, Holmes and I were beset by one constable after another, eager to shake Holmes' hand. Some of them remembered working with Holmes on this case or that. A well-timed glance at my friend told me that he was enjoying every minute of his newfound fame.

Finally, like a ghost, silver haired Commissioner Carruthers appeared out of the crowd and led us up to the stage. I was seated at a table in front, with three other constables and their wives as the Commissioner quieted the band and told people to take their seats. Then he introduced Holmes and the hall erupted in exuberant cheers and applause lasting sixty whole ticks. There was complete silence during his speech, except for the moment when a tardy constable rushed into the hall and seated himself at a table in back. Holmes hesitated a moment, took notice of the interruption, so quickly I doubt anyone except me noticed, then he finished his speech with kudos to Commissioner Carruthers and the good constables of London proper. That brought the roof of the event hall down with applause, cheers and whistles, this time lasting ninety whole ticks.

The five piece brass band started up again as Commissioner Carruthers, knowing Holmes preferred to make his exit, again led us through the crowd of hand-shakers and back-patters. Near the doors, that tardy constable greeted us, his hand outstretched. Holmes took the young man's hand and shook it briskly. But what struck me about the man was the pale and glossy tint his face held and there was a small purple bruise on the left side of his chin. I'd seen this paleness on the faces of many fever victims over the years. It concerned me so much that I asked him about it.

"I was caught in the rain last night during my rounds and feel only a little under the weather, it's the reason I arrived late. I do apologize," he said in a forced, jubilant tone.

"Is that a bruise on your chin?"

"The bruise? Oh…yes, I had a run in with a drunken laborer last night, just before it began raining. It doesn't hurt as bad now. I'm fine, really, Doctor Watson."

"You know me then?" I asked, not recalling the man's features at all.

"Of course he does, Watson," Holmes interrupted matter-of-factly, still grasping the constable's hand. It seemed to me a prolonged hand shake. Then I caught just the briefest glint of suspicion in his eyes as he stared at the man. "This is Constable Richard Avery, he along with Commissioner Carruthers and a pair of other constables helped us catch the Black Rose Ruffians two years ago, remember?"

I glanced at the man again and it all came back to me. The Black Rose Ruffians were a gang of kidnappers, holding wives of the wealthy for huge ransoms. Constable Avery, his family going back seven generations in England, had reported his wife kidnapped by them. It was only because of Holmes' brilliant deductions that Scotland Yard found them, broke the gang up, and secured Avery's wife unharmed.

"And how is your wife…Camilla, is that correct?" Holmes asked, pretending for some reason to find it hard to remember her name.

Young Avery nodded, blinked his eyes quickly and answered. “Very well, sir.” His answer didn’t sound convincing to me at all, but apparently Holmes hadn’t heard the answer, which was strange because I’ve seen him track a cricket down in a field from fifty yards away. He leaned in closely, his nose nearly touching Avery’s neck, and asked him to repeat his answer. In a louder voice, Avery said, “Very well, sir! Thank you!”

“Good, good,” Holmes said. “Is she here tonight?”

“No, sir,” Avery replied, he was sweating profusely now, his skin growing so pale it seemed transparent. That purple bruise on his chin was disappearing right before my eyes. I thought he was going to faint straight out. “She’s visiting her cousin in Cornwall. But she sends her good wishes to you.”

“That’s very nice of her,” Holmes said as he politely pulled away from Avery’s neck and released his hand, but not without a quick look at the constable’s fingers. Then he flashed a glance down at Avery’s boots. Something was going on right in front of me but I didn’t know what it was. Why was Holmes acting so strangely? What was all this suspicious inspection about?

Commissioner Carruthers looked as in the dark as I was.

"Tell me, Constable Avery," Holmes began. "When did your wife leave for Cornwall?"

"Uh…two days ago, sir. Wednesday. I put her on the steamer in Paddington Station two days ago. Yes, that's right."

"Hmmm. I would love to go up to Cornwall and visit her. See if she's completely recovered from that horrible event of two years ago. Do you think she'd mind?"

"Uh…not at all, sir. But she'll be back in three days, you could call on us then, at Averyshire. I think that would be better."

"I see," Holmes said flatly. There was a long, uncomfortable silence between the two men, most of which Avery spent refusing to make eye contact with Holmes. "As I recall, your wife has blond hair, does she not?"

"Yes-yes, sir. That's correct." Young Avery was trembling like a plucked violin string now.

Holmes reached out, fingered something on Avery's jacket, then pulled his hand back. In between his fingertips was a single strand of blond hair. Holmes brought it up to his nose and sniffed it. "Commissioner Carruthers," he said. "I think it proper that you arrest this man."

The Commissioner's face went red as a carpet burn. "Arrest him? Avery? For what?"

Holmes' eyes settled directly into Avery's and a slight, knowing grin creased his face. "For the murder of his wife, Camilla."

***

"I say, Holmes," I began, flummoxed to gills. "You never cease to amaze me."

"It was all very elementary, my dear Watson," Holmes said, for the first time ever.

We were standing outside the confession box in Scotland Yard, where through a window we could see Constable Avery sitting at a table weeping into his hands. He'd just confessed to strangling then burying his wife in the forest outside the grounds of Averyshire, the castle that had been kept in his family for seven generations. It had been a crime of passion. He'd been having an affair with a Lady from another well-to-do family and Camilla had found out. She threatened to divorce him, make everything public at the fundraiser that night, destroy his family name and wreck his wealth. A wealth that was willed to him only if he promised to take a menial job, learn what the true importance of having money was all about, that's why he'd become a constable. While constables were digging up Avery's wife, Avery's father, approaching seventy years old, had been notified of his son's crime and was on the way with a barrister. Commissioner Carruthers was reading the confession Avery had written, shaking his head in disbelief, his face still red.

"But what made you suspect?" I asked Holmes, nearly delirious with curiosity.

"It all began with you, Watson."

"Me? What did I do, Holmes?"

"It was you that brought attention to Avery's ill countenance," Holmes explained. "You logically assumed his paleness was caused by yellow fever. But remembering that we're in late October now and it's too cold for mosquito's to live and breed and spread yellow fever, his paleness had to be caused by another factor. He claimed it was by being caught out in the rain and he caught a slight chill, but if you remember, Watson, it hadn't rained last night - it rained yesterday morning."

"Yes, that's right! I remember we went out to pick up our tuxedos for tonight. It was a clear and starry night!" I exclaimed.

"Proving Avery lied and when someone lies, he's hiding something. Leading me no other choice but to deduce that his paleness and clamminess were caused by exertion. But exertion from doing what? While shaking his hand I felt a number of fresh, thick calluses, the kind only brought on by digging with a heavy shovel. A quick look at his fingernails showed that there was fresh soil underneath them. Another quick look at his boots proved that they hadn't been shined, but were covered in a thick layer of dirt. So then I wondered; why was he digging as recently as an hour before arriving to the event hall? Which led me to the bruise on his chin, also fresh in every aspect. I'm sure when Commissioner Carruthers looks up Avery's work schedule, he'll find that Avery was off last night. The violent drunken laborer was an invention. I surmised that he received the bruise earlier tonight, but from who?"

"Who indeed?" I asked incredulously.

"When I noticed that Avery's wife was absent from tonight's event, something no constable's wife would do unless under duress, I suspected it was his wife that had given him the bruise, in a desperate fight for her life, so I started asking him questions about her."

"I remember."

"Then I'm sure you noticed how his nervousness increased, how he began stuttering and sweating. Every answer concerning his wife was a lie."

"All of it? And you know this how?" I asked.

"Easily. Avery claimed that he hadn't seen his wife for two days, that would be Wednesday, yet when I leaned in, feigning deafness, I distinctly smelled her perfume on his jacket. It's called *Misty Mountain*, the same perfume she was wearing two years ago when we rescued her from the Black Rose Ruffians. So she and Avery had been in very close quarters very recently. Then, as you saw, I found a strand of Camilla's freshly washed hair on Avery's jacket. Upon closer inspection I saw that it had been pulled out by the root, during a violent process."

"Pure brilliance, Holmes!" I said, my head was drowning with information overload.

"The kicker was that Avery claimed he put his wife on a Paddington Station steamer heading out for Cornwall on Wednesday, but I've memorized all the train schedules in London and know the Paddington Station steamer only goes to Cornwall on weekends."

"I'm - I'm fumblegutted, Holmes," I said. "Only you could have pulled this off."

"On the contrary, Watson," Holmes countered. "All one has to do is remember to use all his senses when investigating a crime. As I said before, it's all elementary."

A MOST IRREGULAR MURDER

I was awoken from a sound sleep by a menacing thump originating from the parlour of our flat on 221b Baker Street.

Quickly, yet most stealthily, I lit a lamp, put on a robe and slippers then checked the clock on my bed stand, it read just after four in the morn – dawn was only an hour away. I stood next to my bed, listening like a guard dog in waiting, for another disturbance. After a minute of this, I heard nothing more. Still, the memory of that thump rattled me, it sounded suspicious and would keep me awake until I checked it out. I pulled open the top drawer of my bed stand, took out my service revolver. Once I had that cold steel in my hand and checked to make sure all the barrels were full, I locked the hammer back…now I had courage enough to open my bedroom door. I had hoped to meet Holmes coming out of his room, as he is often a light sleeper and may have heard the noise also, but no, my compatriot still slept soundly - his door remained closed.

I held the lamp high with one hand and aimed the revolver forward with my other as I cautiously stepped into the parlour. The rhythmic pumping of my heart drummed relentlessly in my ears, my trigger finger ready to spring at any moment. That was when I saw it…the door to the flat was wide open, revealing the hall and the staircase beyond! Someone had entered the flat! My thoughts went immediately to Mrs Hudson, our good landlord down in 221a, hoping no harm had come to her by way of the mysterious prowler.

I froze and listened again, all my senses tuned and focused. This time I heard a strange sound, almost like a small puppy whining to be let out, it was coming from the floor just beyond Holmes' double wide armchair. With the revolver trembling in my hand, I went around the piece of furniture and saw the object of my quest, lying there in a heap of old, tattered clothes and blood.

It was a small figure, a boy judging from the way he was dressed, laying on his back, arms outstretched, palms open and facing up. His legs were spread apart, his bare feet dirty, almost completely blackened. His chest rose and fell rapidly, in concert with that high pitched wheezing. Whoever it was, he was in a very bad way. It occurred to me that this could be one of Holmes' famous *Baker Street Irregulars*, that band of homeless street urchins we often received aid and information from to help close a case.

I released the hammer on the revolver and threw it on to Holmes' armchair as I rushed over to perform a hurried triage. I knelt down beside the boy, placing the lamp near his head so that I could see properly, but what I saw horrified me. The boy's right eye was badly swollen and purpled, so much so that I couldn't discern where his eyelids met. His nose was smashed in and bloodied, malformed almost beyond recognition; wheezing was coming from his left nostril, the only one of the two that was clear enough to allow air in and out. There was a curious purple bruise on his right side cheek, in what I recognized to be the shape of a small hand with only four fingers, the absent one being the ring finger; obviously the shadow of a very powerful slap. His chin and lips nearest the bruise were grossly swollen and bloody, it was obvious to me his jaw was broken, it wouldn't be easy for him to speak while in that condition. But the worst injury was to his head just above his right temple, it was plain to see that the skull underneath had been smashed in by a hard, blunt object, the edges were sharp and distinctly rectangular. Dark, coagulating blood had caked around the injury in a futile effort to halt the flow. The left side of the boy's face, though, was relatively untouched and for a moment I'd thought him familiar. His left eye blinked twice then he seemed to recognize me as his pupil fell directly upon my visage. He looked to be no older than ten or eleven.

His left arm moved and the fingers of his left hand grabbed on to my wrist, pulling it towards him. I leaned over, positioning my ear over his mouth. With great effort, the boy whispered: "Help…Holmes…help."

"What's your name, boy?" I asked but the only answer I received was a forced sigh. His good eye closed then he released his desperate grip on my wrist. He'd expended too much energy and just lay there, wheezing horribly. It was clear that there was nothing I could do to fix his injuries, it was only a matter of time before he expired.

"Holmes!" I cried. "Holmes! Hurry! There's a dying boy here to see you!"

***

"It's young Peter Lawson," Holmes said as he knelt down next to the boy. The name was familiar but it still wasn't clear to me exactly who he was.

"One of your Irregulars?" I asked.

"Yes, he helped us track down Thornwald, that damned giant who stole the Pearl of Death last year, remember?"

I did remember the boy now. Holmes had given him two shillings instead of one, for his services. "Do you think the pearl has anything to do with this?" I asked.

Holmes was scanning the dying boy from head to toe, he had a disgusted grimace on his face. "Not at all, Watson. Thornwald died falling through that roof and the pearl has been returned to the proper authorities. That case is closed. Young Master Peter has been beaten for an entirely unrelated reason."

The boy, hearing Holmes' voice, came out of his stupor and looked up at the consulting detective with a clear, concentrated eye. His energy seemed replenished.

"Peter," Holmes began. "Can you speak? Who did this to you?"

The boy tried courageously to get his jaw and lips to coordinate but all he could get out were a series of tortured mumbles. Finally he gave up, realizing it was useless. With his left hand he pointed at the four-fingered bruise on his cheek, then he dropped his hand and moaned. I noticed the boy's breathing becoming shallower and shallower.

"Is there nothing you can do, Watson?" Holmes asked.

"I-I'm sorry, Holmes," I said. "His injuries are far too-"

"Never mind! I have something," Holmes said impatiently, stood up then rushed into his bedroom. A moment later he came out with a small bottle and a hypodermic needle. He knelt down next to the boy again then began pulling the clear liquid from the bottle into the hypodermic. "From my own personal stock," Holmes added. "To ease his suffering."

When he put the bottle on the floor, the label read *Morphine*, evidence of Holmes' continuing struggle with addiction. He plunged the needle into the boy's right arm and pushed the plunger. Young Peter's relief was immediate, but he was going fast.

"Peter," Holmes pleaded as he dropped the needle. "Try to concentrate, try to gather up the strength to answer my questions. I promise I'll find who did this to you, but I need your help for only a few minutes longer…"

In answer, the boy reached into his pants pocket with his right hand and came out with a fist. He thrust his fist into Holmes' hands, opened it, immediately I heard a metallic tinkling sound. Then the boy gave out one last gasp and fell limp, his breathing completely ceased. I took the boy's wrist and felt for a pulse, finding nothing.

"He was so young," I said, shaken to the core at the tragedy I'd just witnessed. "Who would do such a monstrous thing?"

"A devil," Holmes murmured, I could see immense grief masking his face like a cloud of black smoke. "A soulless, evil, unfeeling devil with no regard for human innocence. It's a terrible time we live in, Doctor."

A moment of deep silence passed between us as we slowly let the sad occasion of the past few minutes sink in, though, I suspected Holmes' mind was racing like a stallion at Pemblebrook.

"What did Young Peter give you, Holmes? A clue?"

My voice startled the great consulting detective out of his musings. "What? Oh, this," Holmes answered as he opened his hand. In his palm were two shiny shillings. "I believe, my dear Watson, that Young Peter has hired us to find his killer."

***

As Mrs Hudson went to fetch a morgue wagon and an inspector from Scotland Yard, the sun was coming up, promising yet another overcast and dreary spring morning in London. Holmes ran a glass over Peter's corpse many times, looking for the most miniscule evidence of the boy's plight. I did what I could to assist him but I was still deeply troubled and fear I was only hindering his investigation.

“Ah, what’s this, then?” Holmes said as he focused in on Peter’s head wound. He used a pair of tweezers and pulled something from the blood and gore.

He held it up for me to see but I could only guess what it was and told Holmes so: “It resembles a sliver of some kind.”

“Quite correct, my friend,” Holmes said as he spun it around in front of his piercing brown eyes. Then he brought it to his nostrils and sniffed. The repugnance of this made me queasy but I trusted that he knew what he was doing. “Yes. A cedar sliver to be exact, a wood commonly used in ship building, which places Young Peter’s mauling near one of the ship building yards on the banks of the Thames, somewhere in the East End.”

The logic of this deduction was unshakeable, but he had more.

“I’d say the murder weapon was a piece of wood, not a very common choice when it comes to killing. It was probably lying conveniently near the attacker, which means Peter’s killing wasn’t premeditated. It was spur of the moment, fueled on by high tempers and a vicious argument. Judging from the distinctly shaped wound, it was a two-by-four or something very close to that size.”

I stared at the wound and shook my head. "It's truly amazing to me, Holmes," I began. "That the boy could reach our flat from the East End with such a debilitating injury."

"It's not amazing at all, Watson," Holmes stated calmly. "The last desperate action of Young Master Peter's life was to get here, it tells you how important it was for him. In all of London, our flat was the place he chose to die. If we are to catch his killer, there is no better place for him to go and he knew that."

"Is there anything else you can discern from his corpse?"

Holmes nodded. "All the bruises and wounds are on the right side of his face," he said and pointed to the obvious damage. "His killer was left handed. And look at this-" he put his hand close to the mysterious four-fingered bruise. "See how much smaller the killer's hand is compared to mine?"

"The killer was a child?"

"Or a woman."

"A woman? I find that unbelievable, Holmes!" I exclaimed.

"A woman isn't capable of killing, Doctor?" Holmes asked rhetorically. "History is rife with women who kill."

"But in this violent a fashion?"

"Hmmm. I'll give you that, my friend," Holmes conceded as he rubbed his chin. "Usually they poison their victims or hire someone to complete the task. Only prudent, determined investigation will win that debate, Watson. Luckily, we have a four-fingered clue to lead the way!"

***

Detective Inspector Lestrade and the wagon men from the morgue arrived not long after we'd completed the investigation of Young Peter Lawson's corpse. On the street, outside the flat, as I gave Lestrade the details of the happenings earlier that morning, I noticed Holmes acting strangely. He seemed distracted by things in the shadows of nearby alleys or behind the corners of buildings, things I couldn't see for myself.

Once Lestrade and the morgue wagon left, Holmes came up to me and grabbed my sleeve. "Prepare some tea, milk and biscuits, Watson," he said into my ear. "We're going to have visitors."

I'd long learned not to trouble myself with Holmes' way of mystery, knowing things always became clear to me later on, so I shrugged my shoulders and did as he'd requested. As I boiled the water in the pot, Holmes reclined in his armchair while smoking a pipe, legs crossed - quietly, calmly, perusing through the morning edition of the London Gazette. With the first rising whistle of the tea pot, Mrs Hudson knocked and entered our flat.

"Callers, Mr Holmes," she said. "A whole slew of them."

Holmes quickly folded the gazette, threw it on the floor and stood up. "Thank you, Mrs Hudson," he said. "Please show them in."

As I placed a tray full of biscuits on the dining table, a small army of children came through the door, all were shoddily dressed, very grief stricken and in desperate need of a bath. They were of all shapes and sizes, but none over the age of twelve. The tallest and, in my estimation, oldest of them was a blond haired girl, the only girl in the group, she seemed to be their leader. I couldn't help but be impressed with her raw beauty and strength, she would have made a fine young vision in a different circumstance, a different world.

Holmes stared at them with sincere concern, then finally spoke: "My deepest sympathy for the loss of your compatriot, Irregulars."

The only one not staring hungrily at the biscuits was the girl, she responded in a proper, refined, cordial manner which belied her physical appearance: "Thank you, Mr Holmes.

You've always been fair and good to us in our dealings together, that's why we've come to you this morning."

Holmes, observing their eyes, motioned toward the dining table. "Let's not begin our conversation on an empty stomach, Miss Elsiebeth. Would you all care for a biscuit?" he asked.

Their sad faces brightened and their eyes grew wide as they gratefully nodded and took one biscuit each. Holmes nodded at me to bring in the tea and milk. Only the girl preferred tea, but they all ate and drank eagerly, as if this had been their first meal in days. My heart aching, I also put out a tray of bread and apricot preserves. Holmes smiled as they enjoyed this rare free meal.

Once their stomachs were filled, Holmes led Miss Elsiebeth to my chair and asked her to sit down. He sat down in his armchair, crossed his legs again and rested his chin on his fingertips while the others sat where they could find room on the floor.

"We want you to know that, even though none of us knew Peter very well, we are at your service to help find his killer, Mr Holmes," Miss Elsiebeth began. "Free of our mandatory charge, of course."

“I cannot consider ever receiving your services for free, Miss Elsiebeth,” Holmes retorted. It was the proper sentiment and sat well with them. “You put yourselves in danger when I seek your aid, I only wish I could afford a higher stipend. Now, you said that none of you knew Young Master Peter Lawson very well…then why do you wish to catch his killer?”

“Because he was one of us, sir. All we have out there is each other and we know that if *we* don’t seek justice for wrongs done to us, no one else will. Do you understand that, Mr Holmes?”

“Of course,” Holmes said. “Do any of you know if he had any family? A mother, father, brother or sister?”

Miss Elsiebeth shook her head. “Peter was a loner, Mr Holmes. We didn’t even know his last name until you mentioned it a moment ago.”

“I see. Are any of you familiar with a child or a woman with only four fingers on the left hand – the ring finger being the absent one?”

All the children shot each other quick, confused glances.

“I’m afraid not, sir. But we will do what we can to learn what we can, then pass it on to you.”

"Good. I will be touring the East End later today," Holmes said, which was news to me. "I will keep my ears and eyes open for you and will return the favor."

"Thank you for granting us audience, sir."

All the children, sensing the meeting was over, began standing up.

"Before you leave, Irregulars," Holmes said as he rose from his chair. "I want you to know that my allegiance is with you, I won't rest until this case is closed. And you can trust that I would do the same for each and every one of you."

They nodded and Holmes offered them a biscuit for the road as they left. Once the flat had been vacated, Holmes turned to me. "Come, my friend," he said. "We must disguise ourselves!"

***

By mid-morning our disguises were complete. Holmes forbade our regular daily shaves, thereby adding a rugged roughness to our normally smooth and pristine faces, then he tousled up our hair, adding to that roughness. Next, he raided his costume closet for shabby suit coats and pants that a common man wore in the East End nowadays. Donning a pair of the oldest shoes we each possessed completed the façade. When the reveal was over, I barely recognized Holmes and I'm sure it was the same with me. We could now travel through the dim grime of London's East End without causing suspicion among the natives.

Following Holmes' earlier supposition, we took a hansom to Cable Street, got out and began walking the dingy streets of the East End, heading for the ship building yards on the banks of the Thames, in the Shadwell District. But as we made our way past Farmer Street, Miss Elsiebeth, knowing our identities quite intimately, spotted us with her sharp eyes. She came up and handed Holmes a folded piece of paper.

"It was waiting for me on my cot in the Farmer Street train station when I came back from your flat this morning," she explained.

Holmes unfolded the paper and read it. Immediately his eyes went wide. "I was right, Watson," he said and handed me the note. "We're looking for a woman."

I read the note, in a primitive, uneducated scrawl, it said: *Justis for Petr. Fynd her in th' box!*

"But this reference to the box," I began. "What does it mean?"

"There's an alley on the banks of the river that connects to Wapping Street," Elsiebeth said. "We call it Box Alley because it's lined with small, square flats that cater to men's-"

“You mean it’s a den of prostitution?” Holmes interrupted.

Elsiebeth nodded. “For the ship builders and sailors,” she said.

Holmes must have noticed my extreme reaction and put his hand on my shoulder. “Are you up to this, my friend?” he asked. “You may see things you’ll never be able to forget.”

He was right. I’d heard of horrible places like Box Alley but had never seen them, preferring to keep my nose above the water. Yet I couldn’t abandon my compatriot now that we had a true lead. I’d have to put aside my repugnance for Young Peter’s sake.

“I’m up to it, Holmes,” I said.

Holmes gave me a brisk pat. “Good man,” he said then turned to Elsiebeth. “Can you tell us where this Box Alley is?”

“I can do better than that, sir,” she answered. “I can show you.” She pointed to the entrance to the Farmer Street train station, where she lived, then led us inside. At the entrance we were met with a giant map on the wall that displayed all of Upper and Lower Shadwell, Elsiebeth pointed out our destination.

“Fascinating,” Holmes said. “Watson, do you see what I see?”

Indeed I did. Box Alley lay a block to the west of a ship building yard, just to the north of that was the Griffin Street timber yards. I had no doubt we'd find plenty of unused, discarded cedar timbers that would match the injury to Young Peter Lawson's skull.

"Miss Elsiebeth," Holmes said. "I trust I don't need to ask you to stay behind while we investigate Box Alley?"

"That's no place for the likes of me, Mr Holmes, Godspeed to you and Doctor Watson," she replied.

***

As Holmes and I made our way to Lower Milk Yard Street, then south along Star Street I realized I had some questions that needed answering and made them known.

"Holmes," I started. "Who do you think wrote the note – and why?"

"It was someone who knew Peter and the mysterious woman who killed him," Holmes replied. "As for the why, well, the answer to that is in the note…justice."

"And the woman? Who is she and what would be her motive for killing Peter?"

"It's clear she's a prostitute, Doctor, which means her motive would most likely be income-related."

“Income-related? What could a poor, displaced street urchin like Peter have to offer someone?”

“Two shiny new shillings, Doctor,” Holmes said as he pulled the two coins from his pants pocket. He shook them up in his fist, creating a metallic ringing.

“You’re saying this four-fingered prostitute killed Young Peter for two shillings?”

“They go a long way in the East End, my friend.”

I couldn’t argue that point. As he pocketed the coins, we came to Wapping Street and turned east. A few minutes later we came to a street on the right where run-down, dingy, windowless, box-like hovels lined both sides of the brick concourse, all the way down to the green waters of the Thames. The structures were made of aged, weathered red brick, the mortar missing in some places and I tried to guess what they might have originally been built for, but failed.

“Here we are, Doctor,” Holmes said and we turned, following the alley south. It was like stepping into another world, a nightmare world turned upside down and inside out. Women, their faces gaudily made up, their hair tied up high and curly, their shoulders and bosoms exposed, stood in front of open doors hooting and calling at us as we passed by. A few even gave us a verbal menu of what could be done to us for what price as they showed us their stockinged legs. It was appalling and it darkened my view on human existence. I couldn't imagine what it could be like to live as they did, without hope, happiness or pride. It was all I could do not to turn tail and run out of there.

Suddenly, I felt a strong grip on my arm, causing me to halt. "There, Watson, that one," Holmes said in a low voice.

I looked at the woman he was referring to. She was a thin, short woman with tangled brown hair wearing a black corset and long gray skirt. Her face had the lines of many difficult miles imprinted upon it but I don't think that even when she was younger, she'd been menially attractive.

She noticed us staring at her and waved us over. "'Aye, loves," she gushed through a mouth missing many teeth. "I'll take ya' both on for five quid. I 'av the time an' place!"

My skin crawled as I imagined for the briefest moment what she was selling. "You think she's Peter's killer?" I asked Holmes in disbelief, my mind in no way could conceive of her swinging a cedar beam to the boy's skull.

"Look at her left hand," Holmes instructed. I did so and noticed she was wearing a glove. Remembering that it was mid-April, much too warm to wear gloves, it suddenly made sense to me; she was covering a hideous, four-fingered left hand.

***

Her name was Maude Amber Lawson and she was Peter's mother though she'd never married. Eleven years before one of her clients had made her pregnant. She was a damnable woman, full of spit, spite and vinegar. I honestly had never before heard some of the words she threw at Holmes and I as we dragged her in to Scotland Yard. I realized now why Young Peter had turned to live on the streets.

Detective Inspector Lestrade didn't believe she was Peter's killer until we went to the morgue and displayed Young Peter's corpse, due to be buried in a pauper's cemetery the next day. I was shocked at the lack of reaction the boy's mother had as she saw her son lying there on a slab. She did manage a defiant sneer as Lestrade asked her to press her deformed hand to the bruise on Peter's cheek. She resisted like a tigress but Holmes took her hand in his, forcing her to do it; it matched perfectly. That closed the case.

"Why did you do it?" Lestrade asked. "This boy was your son!"

"What's 'is is mine," she spat. "'E wouldn't give 'em to me! A woman's got to eat, y'know?"

"Give what to you?"

Holmes pulled out the two shillings and showed Lestrade. "These," he said. "Two shillings I gave him for help in solving a case last year."

"Had 'em hid from me th' whole time!" she said through a scowl, her eyes never leaving the glistening coins in Holmes' hand. "Imagine, holdin' those two shillings for a whole year without spendin' 'em. So, when I found out 'e 'ad 'em in 'is pocket, I figured, well, if 'e's not going to spend 'em, then I will. But 'e wouldn't hand 'em over…so I sent a plank upside 'is traitorous little 'ed to teach 'im a lesson, but 'e escaped with what's mine before I could get it from 'im,"

Lestrade's face fogged over red, his eyes glowed orange with anger. "Madame, you can be sure that when they hang you, I'll be there watching with glee!"

***

Young Master Peter's funeral was a somber affair even though it was a bright, sunny spring day. As good members of his extended platonic family, the Baker Street Irregulars, one and all, attended. Solemn and respectful in their goodbyes, they each shook Holmes' hand as they left. Holmes had delivered on his promise to them that he would catch whoever killed Peter and they were grateful.

When the digger returned to cover the casket, Holmes and I headed for the cemetery gates, but only got as far as a row of mangled oak trees near a line of marked and unmarked graves. The gates were clearly visible from our vantage point.

"Why aren't we leaving?" I asked.

Holmes, staring at the gates, replied in a monotone voice. "We'll wait here, behind these trees, for a while. See what happens."

He was expecting someone to come through those gates so, curious, I waited with him in silence. Many minutes passed until finally, a thin, shabbily dressed teenaged boy with holed leather shoes and messy brown hair entered the cemetery. He followed the brick path through the gravestones until he stopped at Young Peter's grave. The digger had long since completed his work and the spot where Peter lay buried suddenly seemed a lonely and abandoned place now, all that showed that he ever existed was a small bed of black soil.

"Come, Watson," Holmes said. "Time to shore up the final piece of the puzzle."

I followed him out of the cover of the trees until we came up behind the boy standing at Peter's grave. The boy either hadn't heard our approach or was ignoring it, for he never moved from his space. We stood next to him and I noticed there were tears running down his cheeks.

"Why did you leave the letter with Miss Elsiebeth instead of telling the police?" Holmes asked.

The boy remained in position, his eyes staring down at the grave, as he answered. "I was afraid, sir. My name is Samuel. Peter was my younger half-brother. We had different dads, mine is th' one who cut off our mother's ring finger. She'd been wearin' his band to wed but she was still seein' men that were payin' for it an' he caught her, so usin' a kitchen knife, he cut off her finger with th' engagement band still on it. Since then she hated all men, includin' Peter an' me. I couldn't tell th' police…they would come an' would 'ave believed my mother's lies, then my mother would 'ave found out it was me that told 'em…she would've done th' same thing to me. Y'see, I still lived with 'er, sir, I couldn't take th' chance. But Peter…'e was always more brave, more strong n me, even though 'e was younger. 'E liked livin' out there on th' street, bein' free, doin' for 'imself. 'E talked so well of th' Irregulars an' of you, Mr 'olmes, an' 'ow you gave him those two shillings. I knew if I contacted Elsiebeth, it would get back to you and you'd fix it all like I was never involved."

“Did Peter ever tell you why he never spent the shillings?” Holmes asked.

“’E was proud of them, sir. Said it was th’ first thing in ‘is life ‘e ever earned. Said ‘e would keep ‘em forever to remind ‘im of a good deed ‘e done for someone else.”

“Your brother was a good, lad, Samuel,” Holmes said sympathetically. “I’m very sorry for your loss.”

My heart was near breaking as I listened to the boy tell his story, but my friend shattered it completely with what he did next. Sherlock Holmes reached into his pocket, came out with the two shiny shillings then handed them to the boy.

“These aren’t mine, Samuel,” he said and we left the boy to his grief.

THE ADVENTURE OF THE UNDERWORLD ASSASSIN

1

With a printed invitation to tea in hand, Sherlock Holmes took the weathered, well-traveled stone steps outside the House of Lords by twos with his long, smooth gait. I followed closely behind as the invitation allowed for one guest.

We were to meet Stanley Arthur, newly elected Member of the British Parliament at three in the afternoon at his parliamentary office and from the beginning, Holmes was suspicious that something was up as the famous consulting detective had always made his distrust and disgust of politics known to anyone who knew him, especially to politicians. Something wasn't right. Holmes had never met this Stanley Arthur before so why would he be suddenly invited to tea by the man? Hiring Holmes was out of the question, surely the man would have known that Holmes found it distasteful to service politicians at any level, no matter what the emergency.

For answers, we attempted to contact Mycroft, Holmes' older brother. Mycroft works, in some secret fashion, for the British Government and would know if the invitation was genuine, but we discovered from his secretary that he was attending an important meeting up at Durham University in north eastern England. With his brother currently unreachable, Holmes decided to play the invitation through, see what happened.

It was a mild, but overcast late April day and there were many people flitting about, on, above and below the steps to the House of Lords. When we reached the top, there was a young man wearing a dark suit standing there looking around with his hands clasped behind his back. With the standard of Queen Victoria embroidered on his chest, he seemed to be employed by the government to answer people's questions going in and out of the huge, brick façade.

Holmes went up to the man and gave him the invitation card. "My good man," he said pleasantly. "Where may I find Mr Stanley Arthur?"

The man looked at the invitation then at Holmes. He blinked once and his eyes focused on something in the distance. He raised his right hand and pointed. "Why, that's him there, sir," he said. "Going down the steps. The man with the hat and walking stick."

Holmes stole the invitation back, turned and rushed after the politician. We finally chased him down as he reached the walk at the bottom of the steps. Holmes introduced himself and myself, then handed him the invitation. Arthur was a tall, overweight but distinguished looking man with a thick, silver mustache and a wide, bulbous nose. He stared at the card as if it was written in a different language. "Who are you again?" Arthur asked. "And what's this all about?"

"Well, sir, my name is Holmes and as the card indicates, you invited us to tea," my compatriot answered.

"Rubbish! I've done no such thing!" Arthur said confidently and handed the card back to Holmes. "The invitation is a fake! Now, if you'll excuse me, I'm expected at an ambassadorial dinner very shortly."

As the tall, big man turned, his throat suddenly erupted in a flash of blood and gore. His head jerked backwards, spinning his hat off. He dropped his walking stick and brought both hands up to his throat as he fell backwards into Holmes' arms. Immediately after, a loud crack shattered the calmness of the afternoon air, so loud it made me jump. I'd heard that sound before, many times while fighting in Afghanistan in defense of our Majesty's interests – the crack of a rifle shot. It came from the west, far across the roadway where a large patch of woods resided, and was so loud people everywhere either scrambled away or hit the ground and covered their heads.

"Hurry, Watson! Tend to him! Quickly, man!" Holmes shouted. I looked down and saw him kneeling next to the wounded politician. Arthur's hands were grasping desperately at his throat, which was spewing short bursts of red liquid through the open spaces between his fingers. He coughed, trying to fill his lungs with air, but instead he was flooding them with blood. His pupils danced around frantically, from me to Holmes and back again in endless cycles. There was a definite glare of surrender in them; he knew as well as I did, that there was no saving him. I attempted to aid him anyway, perhaps there was something I could do to help him go easily into the afterlife, but by the time I knelt down next to him, his breathing had ceased and his blood soaked hands had fallen away from the horrible wound in his throat. Those once frantically dancing eyes froze, glazed over and stared away, up into the clouds.

"He's gone," I murmured as I closed Stanley Arthur's eyelids with a gentle sweep of my fingertips.

Holmes, though, wasn't listening to me. His gaze was focused intensely upon that far away area of woods where the rifle shot had emanated from.

2

Detective Inspector Lestrade and his men arrived a short while later, along with the morgue wagon. As Holmes repeated the exact events of what had happened a few minutes before to Lestrade, I noticed that a crowd had gathered, fenced off by a series of constables, and watching with deep curiosity when the morgue officers cleared Arthur's corpse from the walk, leaving a large, circular blood stain behind. Perhaps the spring rain that constantly harassed London would wash it away.

"The shot came from over there," Holmes said, gesturing to the woods across the roadway. "I suggest we search that area, there must be something of a clue left behind."

Lestrade agreed and we followed Holmes across the brick and gravel roadway, skillfully avoiding the ever present gaggle of hansom cabs going back and forth. When we made the woods, Holmes took in a deep breath then exhaled.

"Do you smell it?" he asked us. "The odor of gunpowder. Very strong in this direction."

Holmes led us through an opening in the brush, which was currently exploding with green buds and we came to a lightly treaded black dirt path, following it around to where a large willow tree stood. Holmes stopped, looked east and pointed. “This is where the assassin stood,” he said. “See the opening through the vegetation? There’s a perfectly clear view of the crime scene from here, yet it’s aptly covered enough to hide the assassin from witnesses looking in this direction. Arthur didn’t stand a chance.”

I looked for myself and agreed, yet one glaring detail stood out for me. “But Holmes,” I began. “The range has got to be nearly a hundred and fifty yards, if not more. It’s an almost impossible shot.”

“I agree,” Holmes mused. “And the assassin was a poor marksman-“

“Poor marksman?” I echoed incredulously. “It’s about as good a shot as I’ve ever seen. The assassin landed a perfect bull’s eye in Arthur’s throat.”

Holmes nodded. “Yes, but he was aiming for the heart, Watson.”

I didn’t follow up and ask how he knew that, I probably wouldn’t have understood it anyway. From past experience, I assumed he was, as usual, correct in his assumption. Holmes glanced down at the black soil of the path and pointed again. “Look here…tracks,” he said. “Fresh and deep. They coalesce here behind the tree then take off to the west.” Holmes took out his glass, knelt down and inspected a single foot track. "Size ten, a hundred and seventy pounds, Scotland Yard issued treads on the shoes."

"You're saying the assassin is a police constable?" Lestrade asked.

"No," Holmes answered as he stood up. "I'm saying he's disguised as a constable. Quite clever…if seen, no one would ask him why he's tromping through the woods near parliament. They'd assume he was running his daily patrol beat."

"But it took a rather distinctive rifle to have made that shot and constables don't carry rifles," Lestrade offered. "If someone saw him carrying one, that would raise a red flag immediately and he'd be made."

"You are quite correct, Detective Inspector," Holmes said. "So logic would dictate that he left it here, in the woods somewhere. Somewhere very close." He turned his attention back to the willow tree and followed another set of tracks around to the other side, facing the roadway. "Aha!" he exclaimed.

Lestrade and I went around and saw a rifle leaning against the bole of the tree, the barrel was pointed up and its tip was pressing a folded piece of white paper against the bark.

“Apparently the assassin has left us a note,” Holmes said knowingly.

3

"I must say, Holmes," I said, leaning forward to inspect the weapon. "I've never seen a rifle like that one before."

"And you probably never will," Holmes said as he inspected it closely. "As you know, over the years I've become an expert on firearms manufactured in all parts of the world. This is a fifty-two caliber sniping rifle, with a maximum range of a thousand yards, manufactured by Sharps-Borchardt in Bridgeport, Connecticut, 1878. Which means, of course, that it's American made."

"Our assassin is an American?" Lestrade asked.

Holmes slipped the note from its pinch between the barrel and the bark and unfolded it. "No, Detective Inspector. But he's been there, and recently."

"How can you know this?"

"From the condition of the barrel. As you can see there's no pitting from entropy, no wear patterns on the stock, no deformation on the hammer. It's pristine, brand new, never been fired before, and it's the most accurate long range weapon in the world. I suspect the assassin traveled to America for the sole purpose of purchasing this weapon to use it for this one particular assassination, telling me that the assassin is upper-middle class and has deep knowledge of firearms from around the world, which means he's a reader, hence – very intelligent."

"What does the note say?" I asked.

"Hmmm," Holmes mumbled as he read silently. "Very interesting indeed. Here, Watson, read it aloud for the Detective Inspector."

I took the note from Holmes and began reading:

"Most brilliant and competent Consulting Detective – Sherlock Holmes,

I've watched your career from afar for two years and suspect I've finally discovered someone equal to my talents – a yin to my yang, a white to my black, if you will. So, I've devised a simple contest to confirm my suspicions...let us set mind against mind on a battle field of intelligence and wit – the most dangerous weapons in the human arsenal. Prove me right and innocent lives will be saved, prove me wrong people will die and my search for an equal will continue. The clock is ticking, solve the riddle below and begin the contest...

The ancient rungs of English power and might have been steadily weakened by termites and must be replaced, one-

at-a-time, so that a ladder of anarchy can be raised, leading eventually to a stronger, new order of government sympathetic to the lowly and the meek.

The first rung, as you have witnessed for yourself, has been destroyed – the next rung up the ladder that needs immediate replacing resides in the kitchen of a common man, where glass, pottery and steel hide. This rung hints of royal blood but it is truly, honestly, common to the core.

Time to see if you can stop me, Mr Holmes…it's your move but you have only until dusk. And remember, there is no great genius without a mixture of madness.

Your Respectful Squire,

The Underworld Assassin."

"Incredible!" I exclaimed and handed the note to Lestrade.

"Yes, my dear Watson," Holmes said. "It seems I'm to be tested like a child in preparatory school, except that if I get a failing grade, people will die."

"But why? And by Whom?"

4

"You read it yourself, Watson," Holmes said. "By an anarchist, a madman quoting Aristotle, confirming my suspicion of the assassin's intelligence."

"You mean that last part about genius being associated with madness?"

"Right. But the questions of who wrote the note or why are unimportant at this point compared to the identity of the next man to be targeted for assassination, which is clearly hinted at in the text of the riddle."

Lestrade looked up from the note. "I can't make sunlight out of any of it, Mr Holmes," he said.

"Then you should read a little slower and with a little more concentration, Detective Inspector," Holmes said. "The riddle references where the rung, or the targeted man, resides-"

"Yes," Lestrade interrupted. "*In the kitchen of a common man, where glass, pottery and steel hide.*"

"Exactly. The first part tells us where he is, the second part tells us what he is," Holmes explained, then he pulled the fake invitation card from his pocket. "Now, we must not forget who the first victim was, that will help us figure out who the second victim is, obviously another member of parliament, as is evidenced by the assassin's reference to the next rung up the ladder of government. Let's see, oh, yes, Mr Stanley Arthur, newly elected Member of Parliament from the House of Lords. If you recall, there are two houses of parliament, the House of Lords and-"

"The House of Commons!" Lestrade exclaimed, as if he'd made the deduction on his own.

"Correct, Detective Inspector," Holmes said. "The *kitchen of the common man* refers to the House of Commons. But where in the kitchen hides *glass, pottery and steel*?"

It was clear Holmes already knew the answer but was walking Lestrade and me through it gently, trying to get our brains to work like his.

"*Glass, pottery and steel*," Lestrade echoed aloud, trying to work it out for himself. But when he said it, the answer became obvious to me.

"A cabinet!" I shouted. "*Glass, pottery and steel* are the dishes and pots stored in the cabinet in a kitchen."

Holmes nodded. "Which means that the next victim is a Cabinet Minister coming from the House of Commons."

"But what about the last part of the riddle – the part about *the next rung hinting at royal blood but being truly, honestly common*?" Lestrade asked.

"That, I suspect, tells us the man's exact name," Holmes answered. "For that I'll need to see the current roll of the Cabinet Ministers of the House of Commons. I'll recognize the man's name as soon as I see it."

"I can help you with that," Lestrade said as he grabbed up the American rifle and led us back to the English Parliament building.

5

Before entering the House of Commons, Lestrade handed the American rifle off to one of his constables, telling him to secure it back at Scotland Yard until further notice. As we made our way up the flight of exterior steps, Lestrade told Holmes and I that a roll of everyone serving in the English government is kept in a designated records office in each house of parliament.

The man in charge of the House of Commons office was a short, frumpy, white haired leprechaun of a man named Barloe. Once Lestrade introduced himself and told him that lives are in the balance, the little man's fuzzy white eyebrows rose like two bursts of smoke and he led us into a back room where shelves of bound books lined every wall and a large empty table sat in the middle. A single, uncurtained window on the west wall supplied the only light but it was fading fast. Dusk was quickly approaching. The assassin's next victim didn't have much time.

Barloe lit a lamp then drew his attention to the east wall, a stumpy finger pressed to his lips as he searched the shelves left and right for the proper volume.

"Hurry up, man!" Lestrade pleaded.

Barloe ignored him and continued his search. “Ah! Here we are!” he said as he reached out and slid a thick, leather-faced book from off the shelf. He placed it on the table with such care I couldn’t hear it touch the polished wood surface.

“This is a complete, updated listing of the current members of parliament,” Barloe said as he opened the book and fanned through the yellowed pages. “As you can see, it goes back many decades. A new page is added after every election cycle, the last one took place last year. Here is the list of present Cabinet Ministers, there are twenty-two of them, hopefully, the man you’re looking for is on it.” He came to a page near the back then stepped away so that we could survey the record. In sharp black ink were the different signatures of the following men:

Darrel T Hendrickson

Richard H Cappel

Robert E Hough

James T Martin

Raymond H Tyler

Christopher I Walstraff

Jacob R Stone

Major T Brish

Thomas E Markey

Charles E Lighterston

Killian N Knight

Manley T Hall

Robert H Earl

George N Ballis

Peter A Wilkerson

Stephen M Rydell

Leslie E Duncan

Alan D Erwine

Randall O Beckwith

Glenn W Sterling

Morris N Dunkling

Leonard Squire

"Do you see him, gentlemen?" Holmes asked.

"My guess is the eleventh man down," Lestrade said. "Killian N Knight."

"Incorrect, Detective Inspector," Holmes said. "Being a knight doesn't necessarily mean one possesses royal blood. Watson?"

"The last name on the list," I stated. "Leonard Squire."

“You two aren’t looking hard enough,” Holmes said. “Our man is the thirteenth name down – Robert H Earl. He possesses the royal title of Earl but is clearly a commoner, just as the assassin’s note directed.”

I felt like slapping myself, the answer was painfully obvious in hindsight.

“Where can we find this Robert Earl, Barloe?” Lestrade asked impatiently.

“Well, being a senior Cabinet Minister, his office is on the fifth floor, sir. Office five-fifteen.”

A quick look out the window told me we had little or no time left. We thanked the short man and hurried out of the room.

6

The halls and staircases of the building were crowded with people, for what reason I couldn't fathom. Perhaps because it was a Friday afternoon and they wanted to get a jump on the weekend. Whatever the reason, it made our trek up to the fifth floor very difficult, even with Lestrade shouting that he was from Scotland Yard and was here on official business.

When we finally reached the fifth floor, the story remained unchanged. The crowds, in fact, seemed even heavier. Holmes was checking the address plaques as we fought our way through the hall. "Earl's office will be on the north side, probably halfway down! Hurry, gentlemen!" he shouted above the rolling din of other voices.

We had had the bad luck to have started out on the south side of the hall so that meant we were to fight and claw our way across the rush of oncoming traffic. No easy task – once, I was nearly trampled by a group of young interns carrying stacks of old books.

Finally, after what seemed like an hour, Holmes shouted "Here!" and we followed him through the open door and into the office where an attractive, professionally dressed, older blond haired woman sat behind a reception desk. There was a large closed oak door in the wall behind her.

"We're looking for Mr Robert Earl! Is he in?" Holmes asked, his voice agitated but steady.

She looked up at us with large blue eyes, suspiciously. "I'm afraid Minister Earl has left for the day, whom my I ask - ?"

Lestrade quickly introduced himself and told her it was a matter of the Minister's continuing life to tell us where he went.

"Oh, dear," she said shakily as she opened a date book that was lying on her desk. She paged through it until she found the proper entry. "It says here that Minister Earl was to meet a constituent in the food commons for tea at a quarter to four and then he was to go purchase a birthday gift for his daughter."

"This food commons...where is it?" Holmes asked.

"I know where it is, Holmes," Lestrade said, thanked the woman and we followed him yet again into the flowing crowd. Pushing, shouting and cursing, we stayed against the north wall as we went east. I could see, at the tail end of the hall, how it opened up into a large room filled with tables, some empty, most full.

"Do you see him?" Holmes asked Lestrade.

"No!" the Detective Inspector answered. "There are too many damn people!"

Then there was a blood curdling scream, coming from somewhere in the chaos in front of us. This lead to a chain reaction of screams, arms flailing about and people running in all directions. Quickly, in their panic, the crowds in the hall thinned out, revealing a tall, thin man with a full head of brown hair and wearing a black suit, standing alone near the entrance of the food commons. He had a briefcase in one hand, his other hand was grasping at something poking out of his chest. A permanent look of confusion was masked upon his middle-aged face. Out of the corner of my eye I saw a black-haired man in a black overcoat running away, down a connecting hallway that led to a flight of stairs. Lestrade saw him too and began pursuit while Holmes and I tended to the man.

The chaotic din of the past few minutes had extinguished itself as people gathered against the walls and watched the proceedings in horror. When we finally reached him, the man pulled a large knife from his chest, his hand and suit covered with blood.

"Are you Robert Earl?" Holmes asked.

The man looked up at Holmes, then at me, holding the weapon out for us to see. "Um…yes, I'm Robert…Earl," he said weakly. It was obvious he was utterly flabbergasted by his predicament. Then his gaze fell upon the bloody knife in his hand. He looked at it as if he'd never seen a knife before, let out a pathetic whimper and collapsed like a balsa wood house in an earthquake. The knife and briefcase hit the floor the same time as his body then he lay there on his back, his chest heaving in rapid bursts.

Without thinking I fell to my knees, tore his vest and shirt open and revealed the wound. It was a straight cut with clean, smooth edges, about an inch and a half long. A slow, steady stream of blood oozed out.

"Is there anything you can do, Watson?" Holmes asked.

I shook my head. "It's right in the heart, Holmes," I replied.

Holmes, knowing what that meant, frowned then turned his attention to Robert Earl, whom was fading fast. "The man who stabbed you," he began. "Do you know his name?"

Robert Earl's eyes bugged out as he struggled to breathe, to live. "Smith," he coughed, blood smattered his thin lips. "John…Smith." Then it was as if time stopped, his body froze and his breathing ceased.

“Well,” I said with relief. “At least we know the assassin’s name.”

Holmes shot me a look of derision. “It’s an alias, Watson,” he spat. “John Smith is the most common name in England. All criminals use it to hide their true identities.”

“Bollocks!” I cursed and slapped a fist into my palm.

“But what’s this?” Holmes asked as he reached forward and pulled a folded piece of paper from Earl’s inner breast pocket. He had it unfolded in a breath. “Just as I thought, it’s another note addressed to me…from the Underworld Assassin!”

7

Lestrade returned at this moment, breathing heavily and sweating profusely. "The assassin...he escaped," he stammered. "Too fast…had his route…planned out…ahead of time."

"Yes," Holmes said. "He's much too clever to be caught out in the open. But he's left us another riddle. Another person's life hangs in the balance."

"Read…read it aloud, Holmes!" Lestrade urged as constables rushed into the food commons to tend to Earl's lifeless corpse.

"Mr Holmes,

Another rung on the rotting ladder of the English government has collapsed. Your tardiness in preventing Minister Earl's death disappoints me to no end. I wonder, now, if you are worthy of our contest – have I chosen my arch adversary incorrectly? I shall give you one more chance. Redeem yourself, sir, for I have upped the ante and now the fate of the entire British Empire relies on your cleverness.

The riddle below betrays the where and who of your next challenge. Solve it if you can:

At this very moment old friends and close family are gathering north and east under the purple banner of three lions and a cross. Since 1832 Fundamenta eius super montibus sanctis, to get there before the scepter and crown falls you'll have to travel Knight and day, extinguish the flame with a short fuse and avoid powder burn.

There, you are officially invited, Mr Holmes, to my party within a party and it's sure to be an explosive affair. Do be punctual this time.

Your Ever Respectful Squire,
The Underworld Assassin"

"The insolence of the man!" I exclaimed. "He cares not a whit for human existence or the goodness of the British way of life!"

"Focus, man!" Holmes demanded. "Or the lives of Arthur and Earl will have been lost in vain! Now, the riddle speaks of *old friends and family gathering north and east under the purple banner of three lions and a cross* – obviously a royal crest of some sort, but for what?"

Lestrade and I exchanged blank glances, both of us clueless as to the meaning of the crest.

Disappointed, Holmes waved his first question off. "We'll return to that. Let's move our attention to the part written in Latin – *Since 1832 Fundamenta eius super montibus sanctis,* which translates in English to '*Her foundations are upon the holy hills.*' Does that spark anything in your minds?"

"Why, yes, of course, Mr Holmes!" Lestrade said. "That's the motto for Durham University, it's the third oldest university in England. The year 1832 is when it was granted a Royal Charter, hence the purple banner of three lions and cross – purple is the hue of the British monarchy!"

Holmes was surprised at Lestrade's outburst. "And Durham University is in the north east of England. How is it that you know so much about this university, Lestrade?" he asked.

"Security purposes, Mr Holmes," Lestrade replied. "You see, Commissioner Carruthers is receiving his knighthood from the Queen on Saturday afternoon in the university's cathedral, all the leaders of parliament are there with her. I was put in charge of coordinating security for the Commissioner during his journey up to Durham County."

"That explains the *old friend* reference, the misspelling of *night* with a *'K'* and the part about the *scepter and crown falling* – a clear reference to the Queen," Holmes said bitterly. "But tell me, Lestrade, why aren't you up there with Carruthers?"

"I-I don't know, Mr Holmes. I'd assumed I'd be going along but my orders were changed at the last minute."

"I sense a puppet master pulling strings behind the scenes," Holmes mused aloud. "All of this theater is designed to lead to the assassination of the Queen – the true target of the Underworld Assassin."

"But how can it be done?" I interrupted. "The Queen is protected by an army of soldiers."

"They'll do her little good if they're dead also. Remember the riddle, Watson? We must *extinguish the flame with a short fuse and avoid powder burn?* I suspect the Underworld Assassin has the entire cathedral rigged with kegs of gunpowder attached to fast fuses, all expertly hidden. How convenient for him that the Queen, along with all the leaders of parliament, are gathered together in the same room at one time. A single massive blast will wipe out the monarchy and the current government all at once, creating a power vacuum...anarchy and bloodshed will sweep over the island in days. It will be a historical and humanitarian disaster of unparalleled proportions."

"We must get word to them, before-" I began.

"Not enough time," Holmes interrupted. "As the riddle predicts, we'll have to *travel knight and day* to get there in time."

"But we're too late to catch a train heading north and Durham is a four day journey from London by horse."

"Then we won't take a horse, Doctor," Lestrade said. "We'll take a steam ship, get there by tomorrow morning. I know a Captain who owes me a favor."

"Brilliant, Detective Inspector," Holmes said.

"But I must tell you something else, Mr Holmes," Lestrade said. "It's about the one thing in the riddle we haven't yet covered – the reference to *close family*."

Holmes stared at him expectantly.

"It's your brother Mycroft... he was ordered by the Queen herself to attend the knighting!"

8

Holmes and I met Lestrade at the Blackfriars Pier on the north side of the Thames just after midnight. A mid-sized steamship named the *A.C. Doyle* waited for us in the water, her single smoke stack coughed white smoke into a foggy black sky, which meant her boiler was primed and ready to go. She was a rusted, unclean and old ship and I was concerned she didn't have it in her to complete our mission.

"Not to worry, Doctor," Lestrade said, noticing my reticence. "She's an able and reliable ship. She'll get us to the docks at Hartlepool sure enough."

"But in time, Lestrade?" I asked.

Holmes laughed at my concern and gave me a reassuring pat on the shoulder. "Relax, my friend," he said. "Have faith in the durability of human engineering."

So we boarded and met the Captain. He was an older, distinguished looking man wearing a white coat, hat and neatly trimmed mustache. His handshake was strong and confident, his solid, commanding baritone voice supported this. Crew members dressed in white shirts and black breeches scurried busily all over the ship, doing whatever it was they were trained to do.

“Welcome aboard, gentlemen,” the Captain said. “My name is Gallagher. Detective Inspector Lestrade has informed me of the importance of your mission.” He looked up into the sky and frowned. “Looks as if a fog is rolling in, I suggest we set off immediately. My attendant will show you to your quarters. If all goes well, we’ll arrive at our destination by nine in the morning.”

“That’s cutting it a little close,” I said. “We have a two or three hour hansom ride after that.”

“Would you prefer to go to Durham by horse?” Lestrade asked rhetorically.

The attendant came up and led us down into the creaky bowels of the ship and to our rooms. The cabin was a small, cramped space with white walls, a single cot in the corner, a bed stand, a lit sconce above that and a sink under a circular porthole on the outside wall. As I sat down on the cot I heard the engines ramp up and felt the ship lurch forward. Holmes and Lestrade were in the cabins on opposite sides of mine and I must say it felt reassuring to have them so close. After a moment I lay down, still fully dressed, and tried to get some rest, letting the low drone of the engines set me off to sleep, but it wasn’t to be. For some time I tossed and turned restlessly, my mind never removing itself from the conceivable dangers we faced when we finally raced into the cathedral at Durham University later that morning.

Frustrated and no more tired than I was when I awoke the previous morning, I got out of bed to see if Holmes was having the same problem as I, but when I knocked on his cabin door, I found it open and the room empty. Same with Lestrade's. Hearing voices overhead, I took the stairs up to the bridge and found Holmes and Lestrade standing shoulder to shoulder in the dark peering through the forward viewport. The Captain was at the wheel and was also obsessed with something in the distance.

I stood next to Holmes and noticed he was donning a pair of field glasses. All I could see was the constant, ghostly dance of fog outside. "What's happening?" I asked in a low voice.

"There's a ship about a mile ahead of us," Holmes said. "We've been following it since we made the North Sea. It seems to be following the same course Captain Gallagher plotted out."

Holmes handed me the field glasses. I looked through the viewport again and this time saw the unmistakable flicker of a light through the fog, some distance out. "The assassin?" I asked.

"That's my guess, Watson," Holmes said. "All other shipping but ours has been forbidden due to the fog. Whoever that is, they're in the same kind of rush as we are."

"He's trying to beat us to the cathedral," I said.

"And will probably be successful," Lestrade said. "Captain Gallagher has informed us that, due to the heaviness of the fog, he's going to have to slow the ship down."

"No sense in running us upon a rock," the Captain said. "Where would your mission be then?"

"Damn," I muttered.

We lost sight of the strange light an hour later and when dawn broke, the fog lifted and nothing but open gray ocean lay ahead. To our left, the dark shadow of mother England rose in the distance, shrouded in the morning mists.

"Hartlepool in two hours," the Captain said.

9

As promised by Captain Gallagher, we docked in Hartlepool by nine. It was a grand day with the sun shining in a clear blue sky but there were metaphorical storm clouds gathering on the horizon, centered directly over Durham Cathedral.

Hartlepool was a busy fishing village with a bustling market, so there was no difficulty finding and hiring a local man with a hansom to take us on the three hour drive northwest to Durham County. The knighting was scheduled to be performed at one so that gave us about an hour of leeway.

The driver of the hansom was a man named Olglesvy, he was the same age as Holmes and I, but one could see how the years of working the sea in harsh, unforgiving weather fell hard about the lines in his face. The skin of his cheeks, nose, chin and forehead were wind burned, creating a permanent tint of pink, his hands were thick but bony and scarred from fishing line. I presume getting randomly hired to take three London officials to Durham was like a vacation for him.

Very quickly, we explained the importance of haste in our mission and then we were on the final leg of our journey. Olglesvy and his proud black mare pulled us along quickly, and due to the old, worn springs under the enclosed cab compartment, the ride along the rural dirt roads was a bumpy and uncomfortable affair, especially with three of us squeezed into the cab compartment.

After an hour, I noticed that Olglesvy was still lashing his mare to the same rapid pace as when we had first begun. Extremely worried, I opened the trap door and made it a point to warn the man not to exhaust the animal, reminding him gently that the goal was to get us to Durham in a timely manner.

"Not to worry, Doctor Watson," he said confidently, the rushing wind blowing his long dirty brown hair backwards. "She's a strong, reliable beast. She'll manage. For Queen and country, 'aye?"

Halfway through our journey the hansom suddenly stopped and a loud thud shook the ground outside. Lestrade, Holmes and I scrambled out of the compartment, seeing, to our utter dismay, the mare lying on the ground, her eyes closed, her mouth open, tongue hanging out and drooling blood. Not a sound emanated from her throat. Quickly, I stepped around Olglesvy and pressed my ear against the mare's chest, checking for the thumping sound of life, but there was none. I got to my feet and shook my head in disgust. "The pace was too much...her heart burst."

"We're stranded?" Lestrade asked angrily.

"It would appear so, Detective Inspector," Holmes said. "The Underworld Assassin has claimed yet another innocent victim in his bid to test me." Then he glanced at Olglesvy. "I'm sorry about your mare, sir. If we're somehow successful in our attempt to save the Queen, I'm sure Scotland Yard as well as the British government will reimburse you for your loss."

Holmes was being too charitable to the man, in my opinion. I'd warned Olglesvy not to push the mare too far but he ignored me. Now, because of his stupidity, he was standing over the animal in silence, staring down at it with tears welling in his eyes and we were still an hour and a half away from our destination. Then I realized why Holmes was so patient with Olglesvy; the loss of his mare was the price he had to pay for that stupidity and was punishment enough. There was no need for any of us to berate him.

"Shall we begin, gentlemen?" Holmes said, pointing down the road. Thick woods lined both sides for miles ahead but there was nothing else we could do, staying put and mourning over the animal wasn't an option. "Are you coming, Olglesvy?"

“No...no, sir,” the man said, his once pink, confident face now colorless and grief stricken. “I’ll stay here until someone comes along, take my hansom back to Hartlepool.”

“Good luck to you then,” Holmes said. We shook the man’s hand then we began marching down the road.

10

A few miles later the woods around us opened up and we came across a sleepy little farming community. Holmes suggested one thing; *where there's a farm, there are horses.* And he was right. The first farm we approached held a half a dozen strong looking mounts of various colors in an enclosed corral. It took some skillful talking by Lestrade and a bit of help from the old farmer's wife but the farmer finally agreed to loan us three steeds so that we may complete our journey and save the monarchy.

"For Queen and country, eh, gentlemen?" the farmer said, echoing Olglesvy's sentiment. It was surprising to me how much love and respect the Queen harbored in the hearts of her countrymen wherever we went. She was a symbol of pride and strength to them, and rightfully so as she had expanded and strengthened the might of the British Empire during every year of her reign, making it the most powerful country in the world.

Holmes paid the farmer six shillings as a security fee and we were off. My pocket watch read nearly twelve thirty so it was disappointing that the pleasant scenery remained a blur to me while we raced at top speed to Durham County. Over bridge, through twisting vale, into and out of dense woods we rode, time snapping at our heels, until finally we entered Durham County common and saw the ancient stone spires and weathered arched roofs of the cathedral rising up above the trees not far away. We crossed a bridge that spanned the River Wear and were upon the cathedral in short order. The long, gilded royal caravan surrounded the grounds as if in siege, the horses decorated in gold and purple silken banners, while royal attendants stood watch near them. It was hard for me to believe that our beloved Queen stood just inside the walls of the cathedral.

We halted our mounts then jumped down, quickly being approached by a royal guard, who carried a long snouted rifle and eyed us suspiciously. Once Lestrade introduced himself and pleaded our desperate case, he allowed us to go inside the cathedral where the solemn ceremony of the knighting of our good friend, Scotland Yard Commissioner Yancy Carruthers, proceeded with blissful ignorance.

The three of us made no noise as we entered the vast inner sanctum of the cathedral from a side door. Colorful stained glass windows, many stories high, cut into the high elevations of the outer walls, underneath them were empty, closed confessionals. Candles on tall, golden holders were placed every few feet, spilling the spice-scented odor of candle wax into the air. At the end of every pew row, sculpted marble columns rose up into the ornately decorated ceiling and every pew in the nave was filled, there were even people standing in the side aisles. Every eye was directed forward, towards the base of the pulpit where the Queen stood in all her royal finery, holding a shining long broadsword over a kneeling Carruthers. A choir standing back at the high altar sang a slow, moaning dirge, their voices echoing relentlessly off the countless surfaces in the cathedral. I'd never seen a knighting before and the theatre of it took my breath away.

"The ceremony is nearly completed," Lestrade whispered irritably. "We've not much time. Do you see anything suspicious?"

I scanned the crowd sitting in the pews, the empty confessionals, then I caught the familiar whiff of cigar smoke. Letting my nose point me in the origin of its direction, I saw a black haired man standing alone way up on the second level vestibule, in an opening at the front of the cathedral above the main entrance. He had a cigar in his mouth and seemed to be staring down at the three of us.

"Up there," I whispered, tugging Holmes' sleeve.

"Ah, yes, Watson, well done," Holmes said. "And look, coming down from the edge of the opening in the vestibule..."

I squinted and saw what Holmes was talking about. It was a thin cord of some kind, streaming down from the opening, along the wall and then tightly circled around a sculpted column until it disappeared somewhere under the pews near the rear.

"What the bloody hell is it?" Lestrade asked.

"A fuse, my friend," Holmes answered. "And the man has a lit cigar in his mouth."

11

I considered screaming a warning to everyone to get out but realized that would only cause a panic and probably force the dreadful man to light the fuse. Then I considered cutting the fuse with my handy pocket knife but I was sure the Underworld Assassin had a contingency for that also, like a secondary fuse. It seemed to me it was a final confrontation he wanted so, without a moment's more hesitation, we hurried to a flight of winding stairs near the entrance and rushed up to the second level vestibule.

The man stood there in his place by the window that overlooked the grand ceremony below, cigar still in his mouth and an unconcerned aura about him. The blunt end of the fuse hung by his left arm. He was a medium sized man with a long, chiseled face and black, soulless eyes. The cape was gone, replaced by a black suit and tie. This unremarkable, plain looking man instilled no fear or intimidation in me. I couldn't believe he was the man who'd outsmarted Holmes back at the House of Commons the day before.

"'Ello, Mr Holmes," the man said through his cigar, a deep cockney accent weighed heavily in his voice. When the three of us took a step forward, only a few feet from him now, he reached up with his left hand and pulled the cigar out, holding it very near the fuse. “I knew you wouldn’t disappoint me this time.”

“I’m glad I’ve lived up to your expectations,” Holmes said smarmily. But there was something about Holmes that struck me as odd. His face betrayed a look of suspicion and intense curiosity...and boldness, something one shouldn’t have been feeling when the real possibility of the assassination of the Queen in an exploding cathedral was at hand. “What happens now?”

The assassin smirked and pointed the cigar at my compatriot. “You, Mr Holmes, try to stop me from blowin’ this building an’ everyone inside it, up.”

“But that means you’ll die too,” Holmes said.

“Maybe. Maybe not.”

There was a wide, stained glass window on the outside wall portraying a haloed Jesus walking on the turbulent waters of the Sea of Galilee, the boat with the disciples floated in the distance. Perhaps the assassin’s plan was to jump through the window, to the ground two levels down and escape the blast. Whatever it was, I was having none of it. I took another step towards him.

“That’s far enough, Doctor Watson!” the man spat with a raised voice, but the soaring voices from the choir below still echoed loudly, covering any conversation we were having from those in the pews.

“You’re familiar with me, then?” I asked, trying to spread the conversation out so long that his cigar would extinguish itself.

“An’ also with Holmes, Detective Inspector Lestrade an’ Commissioner Carruthers, thanks to your well-written adventures printed in the *London Gazette*. In my ‘umble opinion, they be the only reason to read that rag, sir.”

“I agree,” Holmes interjected. “Who was it that said; *the man who reads nothing at all is better educated than the man who reads nothing but newspapers?”*

The man stood there, gazing at Holmes with empty, motionless eyes. An answer was not forthcoming.

“You don’t know?” Holmes suggested more than asked. “A man who considers himself a mad genius, a man who quotes Aristotle in deviously written riddles is unfamiliar with a quote from one of the great thinkers of the last century - Thomas Jefferson?”

All that confidence and ease in which the man had stood suddenly disappeared. His expression became anxious and fearful. "What? I...I-" he stammered.

"You're not the Underworld Assassin, are you?" Holmes asked sharply, taking a quick step forward. "No. You're someone who's been hired to play him. Judging from your thick accent, you're from Liverpool or the area surrounding it and you're uneducated, didn't make it past elementary school. That nice new black suit tells me you've been groomed for the part by a secret benefactor. That cheap cigar you're smoking, the distinctive aroma tells me it's from the south of France, the Foulon region I'd guess."

"How...how did you-?"

"It's been my experience that most criminals too poor to purchase the real thing fall back on that particular brand because of the smooth pull, imitating a more expensive cigar; a mad genius would know better and wouldn't sully his mouth on it because the leaves in a Foulon cigar are bitter and mildly poisonous, leaving dark rashes on the lips. What's your name and who are you really working for? How much is he paying you? Who's the true genius behind this idiotic contest? Speak up, man!"

The man, knowing he'd been cornered, thrust the cigar into his mouth to reignite the tobacco. Clearly, it was his intention to light the fuse and take the truth with him into the grave. But just as he pulled the cigar out of his mouth, a man's voice rang out from behind us. "What's going on up here?" it asked. This caused the merest hesitation in the man's desire to light the fuse and I took advantage of it, running into the man with as much force as I could muster, knocking the flaming cigar from his hand. He and the cigar went flailing over the edge, proving once again Newton's long held theory that things under a gravitational pull fall at the same speed.

12

As it turned out, the Queen's sword came down upon Commissioner Carruther's shoulders just as the man and the cigar hit the floor, so there was very little interruption in the ceremony. The disruption of the assassination attempt by Lestrade, Holmes and I won us a personal audience with the Queen before she headed back to the palace in London. She was most grateful for our efforts and threatened to award us with knighthoods but humbly, the three of us declined, knowing we were as yet still unworthy for such an honor.

We took a train with a private car back to London that evening. Mycroft and Sir Carruthers were keen on traveling with us to hear all the details about our adventure of the past two days. Afterwards, Holmes sat in his seat staring out the window, a forlorn look on his face.

"By God!" I exclaimed. "What's wrong with you, Holmes? We've saved the Queen and the empire! We're heroes!"

Holmes shot a quick glance to each of us then answered. "But there's still that one loose end, Watson," he said. "The mastermind behind the Underworld Assassin. He remains at large and just as dangerous as before. Who's to say we won't be going through another adventure like this in a week, month or year from now? And perhaps the next time we won't be so lucky."

"That's a frightening thought, Holmes," Sir Carruthers said.

"But a possible one, My Lord."

The five of us fell into a kind of depressed stupor until finally Lestrade broke the silence. "Let's at least enjoy this victory, even if it is a minor one," he protested. "And worry about that later."

It seemed a good suggestion and we all eagerly agreed. Then a train steward opened the sliding door to our cabin and handed an envelope to Holmes. Holmes tipped the steward. "Did you see who gave this to you, steward?" he asked.

"No, sir. It was in the mail bin when the train left the station in Durham."

"Thank you," Holmes said and waited until the man left before tearing the envelope open.

"Hmmm," he mumbled. "It's from our mastermind, gentlemen."

Without any prompting from us, Holmes read the missive aloud:

"The Great and Formidable Consulting Detective, Mr Sherlock Holmes,

You have proved to be an adequate yin to my yang after all! Congratulations on this accomplishment. You have preserved the English way of life using merely your intelligence – for this I respect you. As Shakespeare once wrote, 'Let me embrace thee, sour adversity, for wise men say it is the wisest course.'

You'll forgive me, I trust, if I'm not choked up about my puppet perishing in that terrible fall, as some loose ends are better left untouched in the end.

You have earned yourself and England a short reprieve, Mr Holmes, but mark my words, we will match wits again sometime in the future. In the meantime, I'll watch your progress from the shadows – planning the steps for our next dance.

Your Ever Respectful (but defeated) Squire,
The Puppet Master"

"Remarkable," I said. "I don't think I shall ever sleep again."

“Come now, Watson,” Holmes said as he slid the letter back into the envelope. “Nothing sharpens a mind like a challenge. I shall be far better prepared the next time.”

“I agree,” Sir Carruthers said. “You are far too brilliant a man to fail. This ruffian stands no chance.”

“Tell me, Holmes,” I said. “Just who was that man that walked in on us in the vestibule, distracting the assassin long enough for us to defeat him?”

“A man who works at the university, Watson. The newest Chair of the Mathematics Department, his name was Moriarty. Professor James Moriarty.”

Also from MX Publishing

MX Publishing is the world's largest specialist Sherlock Holmes publisher, with over a hundred titles and fifty authors creating the latest in Sherlock Holmes fiction and non-fiction.

From traditional short stories and novels to travel guides and quiz books, MX Publishing cater for all Holmes fans.

The collection includes leading titles such as *Benedict Cumberbatch In Transition* and *The Norwood Author* which won the 2011 Howlett Award (Sherlock Holmes Book of the Year).

MX Publishing also has one of the largest communities of Holmes fans on Facebook with regular contributions from dozens of authors.

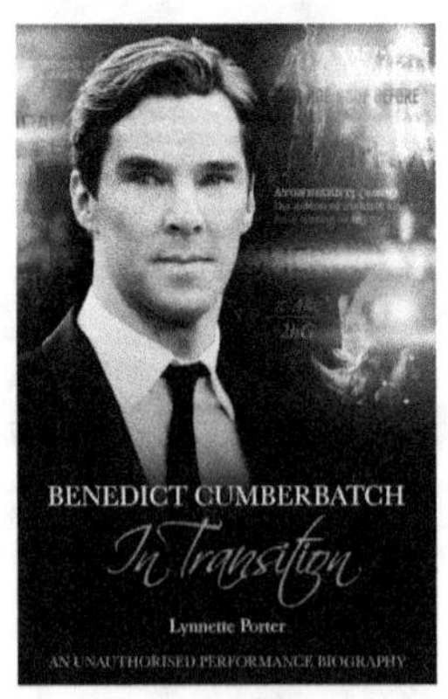

Also from MX Publishing

Sherlock Holmes Short Story Collections

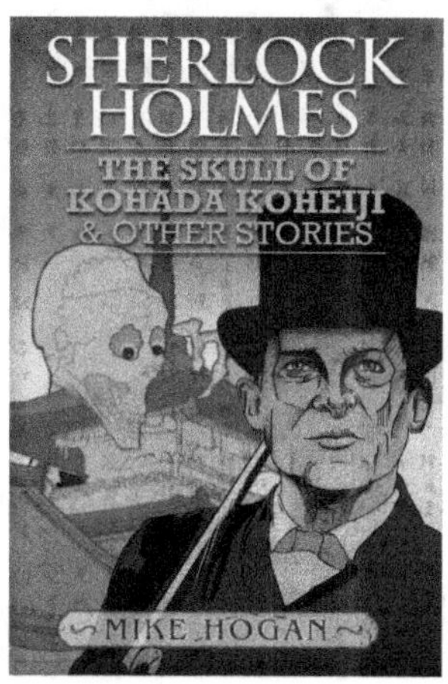

Sherlock Holmes and the Murder at the Savoy

Sherlock Holmes and the Skull of Kohada Koheiji

Look out for the new novel from Mike Hogan
– *The Scottish Question.*

www.mxpublishing.com

Also from MX Publishing

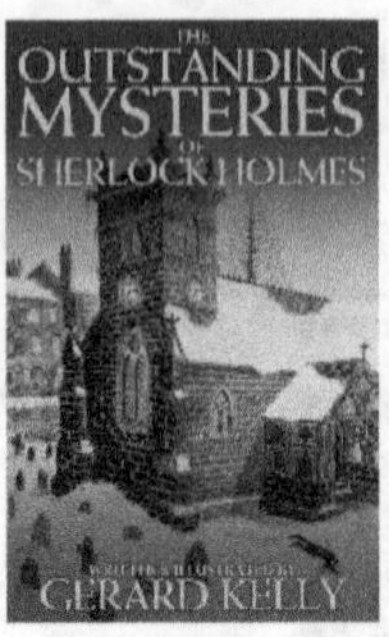

Our bestselling books are our short story collections;

'Lost Stories of Sherlock Holmes' , 'The Outstanding Mysteries of Sherlock Holmes', The Papers of Sherlock Holmes Volume 1 and 2, 'Untold Adventures of Sherlock Holmes' (and the sequel 'Studies in Legacy) and 'Sherlock Holmes in Pursuit', 'The Cotswold Werewolf and Other Stories of Sherlock Holmes' – and many more……

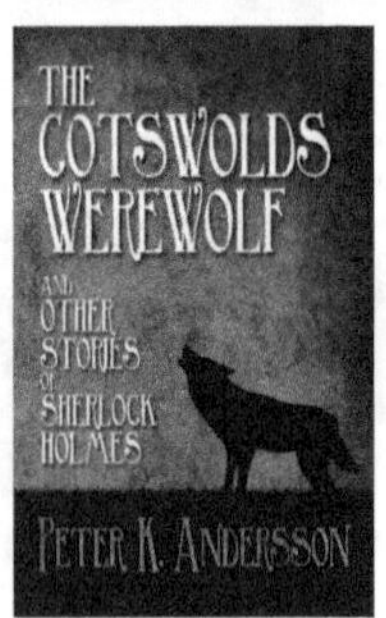

www.mxpublishing.com

Also from MX Publishing

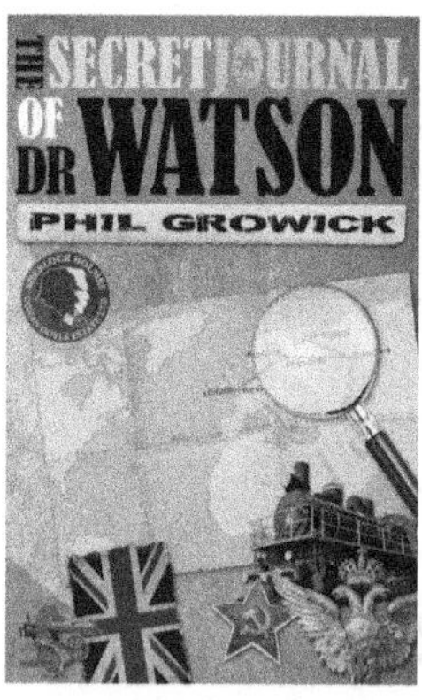

"Phil Growick's, 'The Secret Journal of Dr Watson', is an adventure which takes place in the latter part of Holmes and Watson's lives. They are entrusted by HM Government (although not officially) and the King no less to undertake a rescue mission to save the Romanovs, Russia's Royal family from a grisly end at the hand of the Bolsheviks. There is a wealth of detail in the story but not so much as would detract us from the enjoyment of the story. Espionage, counter-espionage, the ace of spies himself, double-agents, double-crossers...all these flit across the pages in a realistic and exciting way. All the characters are extremely well-drawn and Mr Growick, most importantly, does not falter with a very good ear for Holmesian dialogue indeed. Highly recommended. A five-star effort."

The Baker Street Society

www.mxpublishing.com

Links

MX Publishing are proud to support the Save Undershaw campaign – the campaign to save and restore Sir Arthur Conan Doyle's former home. Undershaw is where he brought Sherlock Holmes back to life, and should be preserved for future generations of Holmes fans.

SaveUndershaw
www.saveundershaw.com

Sherlockology
www.sherlockology.com

MX Publishing
www.mxpublishing.com

You can read more about Sir Arthur Conan Doyle and Undershaw in Alistair Duncan's book (share of royalties to the Undershaw Preservation Trust) – *An Entirely New Country* and in the amazing compilations *Sherlock's Home – The Empty House* and the new book *Two, To One, Be* (all royalties to the Trust).

www.ingramcontent.com/pod-product-compliance
Lightning Source LLC
Chambersburg PA
CBHW071326250626
47159CB00004B/1482
* 9 7 8 1 7 8 0 9 2 7 3 6 7 *